1958

... The blazing torches sent
reflections dancing in the trees like
the shadows of angels. Dust billowed up
around the marchers' feet. Mendy's position,
almost out in the open, meant she could
not move or even flinch without giving
herself away, but her insides
vibrated with fear. . . .

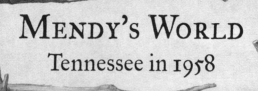

MENDY'S WORLD
Tennessee in 1958

Aunt Sis's cabin

The clearing

Mendy's home

Jeffrey's home

Toward Cowan→

Mendy's home

Main street of Cowan

CIRCLE
OF FIRE

✎

by
Evelyn Coleman

American Girl®

Printed in the United States of America.
01 02 03 04 05 06 07 RRD 10 9 8 7 6 5 4 3 2 1

History Mysteries® and American Girl®
are registered trademarks of Pleasant Company.

PERMISSIONS & PICTURE CREDITS
"Twilight Time" lyric appearing on p. 48 was written by Buck Ram; music by
Morty Nevins and Al Nevins. TRO © Copyright 1944 (Renewed) Devon Music, Inc., New York,
New York. "Twilight Time" Canadian rights MCA Music Publishing. Used by permission.

The following individuals and organizations have generously given permission to
reprint illustrations contained in "A Peek into the Past": p. 141—Photo Archives/AP;
pp. 142–143—Eleanor Roosevelt, State Historical Society of Wisconsin (SHSW),
WHi (X3) 52950, © Highlander Research and Education Center; drinking fountains,
© 1950 Elliott Erwitt/Magnum Photos, Inc.; Jim Crow button, Chrysalis Images;
pp. 144–145—burning cross, © Bettmann/CORBIS (be026735); Myles Horton, SHSW,
WHi (X3) 52947, © Highlander Research and Education Center; Highlander Folk School
in Monteagle, SHSW, WHi (X3) 43722, © Highlander Research and Education Center;
children swimming, SHSW, WHi (X3) 48243, © Highlander Research and Education Center;
pp. 146–147—Highlander students, SHSW, WHi (X3) 52951, © Highlander Research
and Education Center; Rosa Parks, © Bettmann/CORBIS (be031622); Eleanor Roosevelt
with troops, Franklin D. Roosevelt Library and Museum; Highlander today,
© Highlander Research & Education Center.

Cover and Map Illustrations: Jean-Paul Tibbles
Line Art: Laszlo Kubinyi

Library of Congress Cataloging-in-Publication Data
Coleman, Evelyn, 1948–
Circle of fire / by Evelyn Coleman.— 1st ed.
p. cm. — (History mysteries ; 14)
"American girl."
Summary: In 1958, Mendy puts herself in danger when she discovers that
the Ku Klux Klan is planning to bomb the Highlander Folk School
in order to disrupt a visit from Mendy's hero, Eleanor Roosevelt.

ISBN 1-58485-340-9 — ISBN 1-58485-339-5 (pbk.)
1. African Americans—Juvenile fiction. [1. African Americans—Fiction.
2. Prejudices—Fiction. 3. Ku Klux Klan (1915–)—Fiction.
4. Roosevelt, Eleanor, 1884–1962—Fiction. 5. Tennessee—Fiction.]
I. Title. II. Series.
PZ7.C6746 In 2001 [Fic]—dc21   00-069221

To educator Myles Horton,
his wife, musician Zilphia Horton,
children's book author May Justus,
and, of course, Eleanor Roosevelt

These four people risked their lives
for truth and justice.

And to my editor, Peg Ross,
a woman who hears the voices of all people

TABLE OF CONTENTS

CHAPTER I
MENDY'S TAJ MAHAL

Mendy rode hard, her horse's mane flying in the wind, the sting of the air upon her cheeks. *Zoom, boom, crash.* The sounds echoed as horse and rider thundered through the thick forest. Branches snapped, leaves quivered overhead, and the lush-leafed forest yielded to their stampede as twelve-year-old Mendy Thompson rode to her secret hideout.

"Whoa, boy. Whoa," Mendy said when they reached the edge of the clearing. She dismounted her make-believe horse, then bent over and placed her hands on her knees to catch her breath. There was no getting around it—Mendy loved racing through the woods, her heart pumping furiously, the blur of greens, yellows, and browns passing by her like a moving picture.

Mendy breathed deeply. The smell of pine and honeysuckle filled her nose. She took a few more deep breaths and then strolled to the center of the clearing.

There Mendy stood still, her hands on her hips, and surveyed the entire expanse of her land. She was tall, lean, and fierce. A smile quickly embraced her oval, pecan-colored face. There was no doubt in her mind that this forest—and especially this clearing—was the most beautiful place in the whole wide world. There was no place like Mendy's secret clearing.

Well, if the truth were told, this was her land only in her mind. But according to her grandma, all of Tennessee was hers.

Middle Tennessee had been home to a long line of Thompsons. And just like her grandparents before her, Mendy loved its virgin hardwood forests, hills rich with coal, and mineral-laden fields; she loved the nearby town of Cowan, which lay snug in the valley of the Cumberland Plateau. And now, here in this clearing, Mendy had her own piece of land staked out. Like the Chickasaw and Cherokee Indians before her, Mendy felt at home on this land, fair and square.

Just then, Mendy spotted Mr. Hare hopping into the clearing. "Hello, little friend," she said, kneeling in the cool grass and holding out her hand. The furry brown cottontail bounded to her, and Mendy picked him up. She hugged him and cuddled him to her cheek. Then she tickled his plump tummy, making his paws curl under and his ears wiggle. He looked so funny that she laughed.

As she settled Mr. Hare in her arms, she remembered

the day, only a few months before, when she'd saved him from a hunter's trap—her own father's trap, in fact. Now Mr. Hare was healthy and tame. Yes, Mendy thought proudly, when she grew up she would be a "life-giver," just like her grandma had been. Life-giver—that's what the old folks called midwives, the women who helped birth babies and had healing in their hands. Everyone knew that the hands of Mendy's grandma, Lucy Thompson, had burned with healing.

Mendy was glad neither Mama nor Daddy knew where Mr. Hare was now, though. Until recently, Mr. Hare had lived at home with Mendy and even slept in bed with her at night. But then, against Mendy's loud and adamant protest, her daddy told her to let him go free. He said Mendy ought to let Mr. Hare live wild as he was meant to. Mendy was supposed to take him to the woods at the edge of their property, where the locust trees stood, and send him away. But she feared hunters might shoot him, so she had brought him here.

No one hunted in these woods—in fact, no one came here at all, as far as Mendy knew—because mean old Mr. Connor owned the land, and he didn't want anyone on it. That made it the safest place Mendy could think of for Mr. Hare. Everyone knew old Mr. Connor never came out to these woods anymore.

And when she brought Mr. Hare out here that first time, Mendy had discovered the most wonderful, exciting surprise—this clearing right in the center of Mr. Connor's woods. The spot was nestled so deep in the forest that no one could see it from the road. A stream ran near it and caves dotted the surrounding land, making the whole place the perfect hideaway. Since that day, the clearing had been Mendy's own secret place. She named it after the Taj Mahal, a glorious marble palace in India. She'd only told one other person about the clearing—her best friend, Jeffrey. Well, at least she hoped he was her best friend. Mendy wasn't so sure about Jeffrey lately.

Mendy sat down on the tree stump near the center of the clearing and stroked Mr. Hare's soft fur. They watched the shadows lengthen as the sun lowered itself to sleep on the other side of the mountain ridge. Mendy felt safe and protected in the cool stillness of the Taj Mahal. Finally, Mr. Hare broke Mendy's spell by jumping down and scooting off to nibble at a clump of purple wildflowers.

Mendy sighed. It was time to go home anyway.

Mendy scooped Mr. Hare into her arms again. "I'll see you tomorrow, just like always. Now be good, you hear?" Mr. Hare purred loudly. She set the rabbit down and patted his head. "And don't leave the Taj Mahal. It ain't safe in the other parts of this forest."

A hoot owl sounded in the distance, and Mendy reluctantly rose to go. She hated the dusky dark that forced her to head home. With seven kids in the family, there were usually way too many people in their three-bedroom house. Yet now that all her brothers and sisters except Li'l Ben were gone for the summer, the house seemed too empty, and Mama was after her all the time.

Mendy took a few steps toward the edge of the clearing, but Mr. Hare hopped behind her. She whipped around and said loudly, "Stay." Mr. Hare hopped closer. Mendy shook her head at him. She took a few more steps and turned around. Mr. Hare was still at her heels. "Didn't I tell you to stay in the Taj Mahal? Come on," Mendy said, picking up the rabbit by the scruff of his neck. She marched back to the purple flowers. "Stay, now. Don't follow me," Mendy said. "I mean it. Stay." She smiled as Mr. Hare began to nibble the flowers again. Good. It had taken her forever to teach him to stay in the Taj Mahal. Even now, he could be so hardheaded sometimes.

Mendy left the clearing, glancing back only once to see if Mr. Hare was following. He wasn't. Mendy continued down the forest path, wondering if Mama would be mad at her for staying out so long. Then she felt something cold and hard under her bare foot. What on earth *was* that?

Mendy knelt down to look. Suppose she'd found something valuable, like diamonds? Didn't diamonds come from coal? This was coal country, after all. Mendy used a stick to push the forest litter away. When she saw what lay exposed, her breath caught in her throat. It was a burnt cigar, one end dark and mushy-looking, and a plain dime-store lighter. Mendy stabbed at the cigar with a finger to see if the end was as wet as it looked. *Yuck*—it was damp, and it smelled awful.

Mendy stood up and quickly checked the nearby woods for other signs of a trespasser, but she spotted nothing unusual. Still, she knew now that *someone* had been in the Taj Mahal—and suddenly she realized that whoever it was might be coming back. The thought settled on her mind for only a second before she took off running from the woods.

When Mendy sneaked into the house, it was quiet. Usually this time of evening, Mendy's seventeen-year-old sister Clara would be setting the table. Tonight, the kitchen was empty. The older kids—John, Clara, and Morris—had all gone to pick peaches in Georgia with Uncle Phillip, and the eleven-year-old twins, Lilly and Sam, were off staying with Aunt Beulah in Chattanooga so they could go to Bible school.

Mendy opened a cabinet door, careful not to make any noise, and chose a drinking glass. She was sipping the last bit of water and thinking about the ugly, mushy-topped cigar when Mama walked into the kitchen, tying on her apron.

"Where have you been, girl?" Mama demanded. "You been gone for hours. Li'l Ben and I already ate. If Morris was home, I would have sent him looking for you."

A frown sprang up on Mendy's face. She didn't want to tell Mama where she'd been. She was lucky her fifteen-year-old brother Morris wasn't home, because he surely would have blabbed if he'd found her in Mr. Connor's woods; the boy *thought* he was the smartest person on the planet, but his real claim to fame was being a tattle-tale. Mendy didn't answer Mama's question. Instead, she let the empty glass slip from her fingers and crash to the floor. Shards of crystal blue flowers flew across the room.

Mendy's five-year-old brother raced into the kitchen. "Li'l Ben!" Mama yelled. "Stop right there!" Then she looked at Mendy. "What on earth has gotten into you? Why did you drop that glass like that?"

"It slipped out of my hand," Mendy responded quickly as she knelt to pick up the pieces. The glass had been one of Mama's favorites, but breaking it was Mendy's only out.

Mama shook her head. "Get up and go to the living room," she said. "I'll pick it up. Go on, and take Li'l Ben with you."

Mendy took Li'l Ben's hand and led him out of the room, careful to avoid the broken glass.

"You're squeezing my hand too tight," Li'l Ben said.

"Stop whining," Mendy answered. She took him to the couch. "Sit here and I'll read to you." She switched on the lamp and handed him a Bible storybook.

"You in trouble," Li'l Ben said, poking out his lips. "Mama say she gon' tie you to her apron."

"So?" Mendy hissed. "It's none of your business."
Usually the other kids took care of Ben.

Before Mendy had even gotten settled on the couch
next to him, Mama marched into the living room. "Get
washed for supper, Mendy. And you're still gonna practice
the piano before you go to bed."

Mendy headed down the hall and slammed the bathroom door. She heard Mama's warning voice calling, "You
better not slam that door again," but Mendy ignored her.

It wasn't fair. Mama wanted her to practice the piano
all summer so she'd be good enough to play for church.
Once Mama had realized that Mendy could play by ear,
none of the other kids was forced to practice. Mama just
focused on Mendy. Because of Mendy's dumb old musical
talent, the piano was no longer fun. It was a chore, like
gathering up kindling for the fire, shucking corn, or hoe-
ing the vegetable garden. Mendy hated that Mama was so
religious. All Mama thought about was church, church,
and church. Why couldn't Mendy have gone away with
the other kids?

At the dinner table, Mendy was very quiet. She wished
Daddy were home so she'd have someone to talk to. But
Daddy was away working. It was times like these, when
Mendy was alone with Mama, that she missed Grandma
the most. It didn't seem like a year had passed since
Grandma died and left them. Now there was no one to
take up for Mendy if Daddy wasn't home.

Mendy picked at the food on her plate and watched Mama clean up the supper dishes. Li'l Ben had been put to bed. With each stab of her fork, Mendy thought about the cigar and who had left it so close to the Taj Mahal. Had Jeb Connor come out to check his property? No, that cigar could have set the woods on fire; Mr. Connor wouldn't be that careless with his own property. Whoever the trespasser was, Mendy wished she could stop him from coming out there. Scare him off, maybe.

"Mendy," Mama said, interrupting Mendy's thoughts, "first off, stop stabbing that fork on your plate so hard. And second, tomorrow I want you to stay home and help me. Now that the other kids are gone, you're gonna have to help me more with chores."

Mendy wanted to jump up and shout, "Why am I the one being punished all summer?" But instead she silently cleaned off the table.

After piano practice, Mendy sat in her bedroom waiting for her daddy to come home. The room seemed empty without her sisters and Grandma in it. She opened her dresser drawer and took out the scrapbook Grandma had made for her years ago. She looked at the inside cover where her name was printed: *Mendy Anna Thompson.*

Mendy had been given her middle name in honor of Mrs. Anna Eleanor Roosevelt, the former First Lady of the United States. Outside of Mendy, Mrs. Roosevelt had been Grandma's favorite person. Grandma loved to tell

Mendy stories about Mrs. Roosevelt. She even wrote some of Mrs. Roosevelt's sayings inside Mendy's scrapbook. When Grandma was still living, Mendy would memorize them and recite them to Grandma like they were Bible verses. Grandma's favorite was on the first page:

> *Intelligence cannot be judged by whether you are able to read or write; in many cases, this is only a question of whether you have had the opportunity to learn.*

Grandma said she didn't have the opportunity to learn to read and write until she was grown. "Reading and writing is like bread to your soul," Grandma would say. "If you can't read and write, you might as well settle to starve to death."

One day, Grandma had given Mendy an article cut from a newspaper. It was one of Mrs. Roosevelt's "My Day" columns where she told about things that happened to her. Mendy read that Mrs. Roosevelt had always wanted to go to India and see the Taj Mahal, and in 1952 she finally made it.

Later, Daddy gave Mendy a picture of the Taj Mahal to put in her scrapbook. Mendy thought it was the most beautiful place she'd ever seen, with its domed towers glowing in the sunlight. She often dreamed of going to India with Grandma to see the Taj Mahal, riding on the back of an elephant alongside her namesake, Mrs. Roosevelt. Daddy told Mendy that the Taj Mahal had been built for an empress by her husband. The empress had been a brave woman and had traveled with her husband when he went to war. That's why, when Mendy saw the clearing, she had named it the Taj Mahal: it was as if someone had cleared that spot just for Mendy.

Now Mendy wrote on a clean page of the scrapbook:

My Summer in Cowan, 1958
by Mendy Anna Thompson
Today I was lonesome. There was no one to play with but Li'l Ben. I really miss Jeffrey. Sometimes I think he doesn't care that we can't play together no more like we used to. I really miss him coming to the Taj.

Mendy paused. She erased the word *Taj* and replaced it with *woods*. She didn't want to describe the clearing too much in the scrapbook. Suppose Mama read it? Mendy's thoughts went to her Taj Mahal. When had the trespasser been out there? It had to be last night or early this morning; otherwise the end of that cigar would have dried out. Mendy thought, *Ain't nobody got no business out there but me or Jeffrey. Tomorrow I'm going back to see what I can find out.* Then she remembered what Mama had said about helping her around the house.

Well, even if she couldn't get back to the clearing, at

least she and Jeffrey had made plans to meet tomorrow. *It sure will be good to see him again,* Mendy thought. *And I can't wait to tell him about the cigar and lighter.*

Mendy stretched out on her bunk bed. Why would anybody be out there in Mr. Connor's woods in the first place? No answer came to her, and soon she drifted off to sleep.

The coon dogs yelping outside woke Mendy up. That had to mean Daddy was home. Mendy wiped sleep from her eyes and tiptoed to the door of her room. She listened to the front door squeak open, the dogs' yaps suddenly grow louder and then fall silent. She tiptoed down the hallway toward the dark living room.

Daddy sat in the rocker pulling off his brogans.

Mendy whispered, "Hey, Daddy."

"Hey, Wild Trapper," he said, groaning as he stood up and stretched. Daddy called Mendy that because they went hunting and trapping together in the woods. "What is it? I know something's wrong 'cause you whispering. Spill it on out."

"Mama says I have to stay home tomorrow. It ain't fair. I want to go off and play."

Her daddy groaned again and slumped down on the couch. "Sit," he said, motioning to her.

Mendy sat down close to him.

"Listen, you know how your mama is," he said, patting Mendy's hand. "She thinks you need more time with her. That's part why she's sent all the other kids away. So you and her can spend more time together. She wants you to grow up to be a fine lady, like her."

"I don't want to stay here alone, Daddy. She's always after me about something."

"Yeah. That's 'cause she cares about your future. She just wants you to act more ladylike. It won't be so bad. If you stop raising Cain about it and just let your mama have her way, I'll take you out with me some this summer."

A huge grin spread on Mendy's face. "For real, Daddy, you will? You promise?"

Daddy crossed his heart just as Mama called to him from the bedroom. He gave Mendy a hug and said, "Go on to bed now. Count them rabbits and fall asleep."

As Mendy snuggled back into bed, she was filled with thoughts of where she and Daddy would go together. Would they go to their old fishing hole or some new place? Her last thought was that maybe Daddy would take her swimming at the Highlander Folk School in Monteagle. The Highlander School was a place where all kinds of people from all over the world came to study. They were mostly grown people, though. What Mendy liked was that Highlander had the best swimming hole for miles around.

Mendy slept soundly until the morning light warmed

her face through the window. She washed up quickly and got dressed while she listened to the woodpecker drill holes in the grove nearby. The sound echoed in the valley like hammer hits. Mendy loved the sounds of morning.

"Mendy?" Mama called.

"Here I am," Mendy said, joining her parents and Li'l Ben on the porch. All she could think of was her and Daddy's trip.

"I don't want you sneaking off this morning."

"I won't go off nowhere, Mama," Mendy said.

Mama eyed her. "What you up to, Mendy? You ain't gonna whoop and holler about staying home?"

"No, ma'am," Mendy said, catching the wink from her daddy.

"Well, that's a relief," Mama sighed, her shoulders relaxing. "Just for that, I'll give you a treat. I'll let you go across the creek to play with the Hatfield girl real soon."

Mendy smiled back, but she was thinking to herself, *What kind of doings is that?* She didn't like playing with Brenda Hatfield. All the girl knew how to play was some silly tea party. Was the whole summer going to be like this?

Mendy's daddy was going off now to do blacksmithing. He owned a plumbing business, but he still blacksmithed for folks all across Tennessee. He shod horses and mules, built and repaired traps, and fixed wagons. That's why he was gone from home so much.

"Be careful," her mama said, waving to Daddy and

throwing him a kiss as he pulled away in his 1954 Chevy truck. That truck was Daddy's pride and joy. He had saved up his money to buy it, and he had painted the words *Blacksmithing* and *Plumbing* on the side. He had learned plumbing while he was in the army in World War II, before Mendy was even born. Mama often said he learned something else in the Army, too—something that could get him hurt in Tennessee. Mendy didn't know exactly what that was, but she often wondered if learning something new could ever really hurt you.

The minute the truck was out of sight, Mendy went inside with Mama and Li'l Ben. She ate a buttered biscuit. Then she gathered the eggs from the henhouse, swept up the front room, and polished the furniture to a shine. After all her chores were done, Mendy waited for just the right moment—when Mama was ironing and Li'l Ben was asking her a million questions. "Mama," she said, "can I go out for a little while? I won't go far, I promise."

"Yes, but don't be doing nothing you ain't got no business doing, you hear?" Mama said.

Then and only then did Mendy slip away to meet Jeffrey.

CHAPTER 2

PEAS IN A POD

Jeffrey and Mendy had grown up together, and until recently they were like two peas in a pod, as Grandma would say. Jeffrey lived on the next farm over. For years, Jeffrey and Mendy had fished together, hunted together, and roamed the surrounding forest together, hiding out in caves, burying secret treasures, and trying to tame wild animals.

But since Christmas, everything had changed. Their parents had forbidden them to spend time together anymore. They'd said it was because Jeffrey was white and Mendy was colored. Well, Mendy thought, Jeffrey didn't just turn white, did he? Mendy's brothers and sisters could still play with *their* friends, so Mendy and Jeffrey didn't plan on giving up their friendship either.

She and Jeffrey had arranged to meet secretly today at the spring in the Thompsons' woods—which was a good thing since Mama had told Mendy not to leave home this morning. Today was a very special meeting. Last Saturday Jeffrey had gone to the theater to see a new Zorro movie. Mendy had seen the first Zorro movie with her daddy, and she couldn't wait to hear about this one.

Of course, she'd have to deal with Jeffrey acting crazy, but that was okay as long as it didn't last too long. Jeffrey thought he *was* Zorro—the real Zorro—even though they didn't look the least bit alike. Jeffrey had blond hair, sky-blue eyes, and pale white skin, but Zorro looked like a colored man to Mendy.

Mendy was also anxious to tell Jeffrey all about the cigar and lighter she'd found in the clearing. Maybe Jeffrey knew who had been coming to the clearing, she thought to herself. *He'd* better not have brought anyone there without her, though, that's for sure.

Mendy heard Jeffrey approaching through the brush before she spotted him. She whistled one of their new blue-jay signals to let him know exactly where she was waiting.

Jeffrey zoomed up on his bike so fast the tires spun in the dirt, stirring up dust all around him. After ramming the bike smack into a tree, he jumped off and immediately began to swish his imaginary sword.

"Take that and that, you villain," he shouted, one arm thrust into the air, the other hand on his hip. He pranced around until he tripped and crashed over a ground vine.

Mendy burst into laughter. "You're such a knucklehead,"

she said, pointing at him and giggling. "Your mask slipped around. You're going to kill your fool self."

Jeffrey fumbled with the black cloth that covered his eyes. The two slits he'd made to see through were now in the back. "Oh, shut up, before I slash the *Z* sign of Zorro across your chest."

"I'd like to see you try," Mendy said, balling up her fists and taking a fighting stance like her daddy had shown her.

"Put your dukes down," Jeffrey said, "or I won't tell you about the movie."

That did it. Mendy lowered her fists, and they both sat down at the spring and dangled their feet in the cool mineral waters. Mendy listened intently as Jeffrey told her about a duel between Zorro and mean Capitan Monastario on the balcony of an inn, attempting to sound like each character in turn as he described the scene. He told Mendy every detail of *The Sign of Zorro*. When he'd finished, he said, "I'm getting me a black cape just like Zorro's to go with my mask. And I'm going to ask your daddy to make me a real sword. My pa says your daddy's the best blacksmith in these mountains."

Mendy was about to say she would get a mask, cape, and sword, too, when she heard a throat being cleared behind her. Mendy twisted around and looked up into Mama's glaring face.

"I'm going to whip you, Mendy Anna Thompson," Mama said. "It ain't safe for you two to be out here alone—

together. Mendy, I'm going to tell your daddy about this as soon as he gets home. And your parents, Jeffrey," she said, "are gonna get you too, boy."

"I'm sorry, Mrs. Thompson," Jeffrey said, scrambling to his feet. "Please don't tell my parents. Please. I'll never even speak to her again if you just won't tell."

Mendy couldn't believe it. The traitor! They'd vowed the next time their parents said something, they would stick together and just tell them no—that they'd always be friends—forever. After all, they were blood sister and brother. Hadn't they pricked their fingers in the woods, mixed their blood, and recited the oath of loyalty? Mendy felt sick inside.

"Mama," she pleaded. "Why? Why aren't we safe? We ain't bothering nobody. We ain't doing nothing but sitting here on our own land."

"You're old enough to be figuring it out, Mendy. Now let's get going," her mama said. Then she turned to Jeffrey. "You know better, boy. Now go on home. I won't tell your folks this time. But don't let me catch you two again."

"Bye, Mend," Jeffrey whispered. He never called her Mendy.

"Don't 'Mend' me," she shouted. "I don't ever want to see you again, Jeffrey Whitehall. You ain't nothing but a traitor."

Jeffrey hung his head. "I'm sorry, Mend, but my pa—

if he finds out, I'll be in big trouble. That's what he said. Please. Don't be mad at me."

"You just go on home now," Mama said to Jeffrey. "I'm glad you're finally understanding."

Mendy stormed away. She didn't understand anything. How dare Jeffrey promise not to talk to her again? She'd dig up their treasures at the Taj Mahal cave and throw them in the stream. She wouldn't even tell him about the cigar. Boys were nothing but lily-livered cowards.

Mendy had to spend the rest of the morning practicing the piano until she thought her fingers would break. After lunch Mendy asked, "Mama, can I go to Aunt Sis Swain's, since I don't have anyone to play with anymore?"

Sis Swain was the oldest woman around. Mama said that Aunt Sis had been born a slave. Nobody knew how old she was, but Grandma said she was as old as dirt. She wasn't Mendy's real aunt and she wasn't anybody's real sister; people just called her either Sis Swain or Aunt Sis Swain. Sometimes, when Aunt Sis's mind was right, she would answer Mendy's questions as though Mendy wasn't a child but a grownup. Mendy liked those times best.

"I don't want you hanging 'round Sis Swain all the time, Mendy," Mama replied. "She's getting touched with old age. Besides, she needs her rest."

"I promised Aunt Sis I'd come and help her pick blackberries, though, Mama." At least that part was true.

"Well, all right. But I'm warning you, Mendy, you better not be up to anything," Mama said, raising her eyebrows. "Go on, then. While you're at it, you might as well pick enough for us so I can make a pie."

Mendy said, "Thanks, Mama. Are you still going to tell Daddy about me and Jeffrey *just* sitting at the spring talking?"

"Mendy, you are old enough to know that it's not okay for—"

"For *what?*" Mendy asked, sitting up straighter. Maybe her mama was about to explain. It seemed like everyone knew but her.

"Never mind. You just stay away from Jeffrey. That boy is trouble with a capital *T*."

Mendy said okay, but deep in her heart it hurt that she and Jeffrey were no longer blood sister and brother.

Mendy ran almost all the way to Aunt Sis's house. She wanted to see Aunt Sis, but Mendy had another reason for going, too. Aunt Sis lived next to Jeb Connor's forest. When Mendy visited the Taj Mahal, she always went to Aunt Sis's first, so in case she got caught she'd have an alibi.

Mendy picked a few wildflowers as she walked through the woods toward Aunt Sis's house. The house was made of logs with cement between them, and it had a tin roof. Mendy jumped up on the porch in one leap, ignoring the four stone steps.

"Mendy, come on in here, child," Aunt Sis said, opening the door.

Mendy stepped inside. The house had just two rooms. The kitchen and sitting room were all one room, and then there was another small room with a cot. Aunt Sis still had an outhouse instead of an indoor bathroom. Lots of people in the hollow and up on the mountain didn't have running water or inside toilets yet. Aunt Sis lived what people called the "mountain way." She didn't like automobiles or telephones. She did have a small black-and-white television that one of her rich relatives up north had sent to her. But she couldn't turn it on, since she had no electricity.

"Here's some flowers I picked for you, Aunt Sis," Mendy said, smiling.

"Child, you's a sight for sore eyes," Aunt Sis said, even though she'd just seen Mendy yesterday. "You the spitting image of your Great-Uncle Joe, girl. You got them long, tall mountain ways."

Mendy always felt proud when Aunt Sis compared her to Great-Uncle Joe. Great-Uncle Joe was a legend. Why, people said he could shoot a bird in a tree from a mountain away, and he could shoot coins right out of the air. They said he was the best trapper and hunter these mountains had ever seen. Mendy was sure he had loved the woods just as much as she did.

Aunt Sis's voice broke Mendy's thought. "You stop that, now, Caleb," she was saying, gazing toward the woodstove with a faraway look in her eye. Mendy knew what the look meant—Aunt Sis had gotten lost in the past again.

"Aunt Sis," Mendy said gently to call her back.

But Aunt Sis only frowned, still staring in the direction of the stove. "What you doing, Caleb?" she said. "Why you standing there like an old owl? You better quit speaking that African. You know Massa don't 'low it."

"Who?" Mendy said, looking around the room, almost laughing that she'd said *who* just like an owl. But there was no one else, and Aunt Sis was staring at the air on the other side of the room.

"Caleb, quit juking with that stove. Have you got ary sense at all? I can't hardly abide peoples stoking no fire whilst I'm cooking."

"Aunt Sis, the woodstove ain't on and ain't nobody here but us," Mendy said patiently, walking over and lifting the lid of the black iron woodstove. "See?"

"Ahhh, yes," Aunt Sis said, like she'd just sipped a cool drink of water. "Mendy. Mendy, it's you, ain't it?"

"Yes, ma'am. It's me. I came over to help you pick your blackberries today, remember?" Mendy smiled at Aunt Sis. She couldn't understand why grownups made such a big deal of it when Aunt Sis got confused. If you just reminded her gentle-like, eventually she caught on that it was you.

Mendy got Aunt Sis's sunbonnet off the kitchen hook and helped her tie it on her head. She handed Aunt Sis a basket, took one herself, and then guided Aunt Sis out into the back field, where the blackberries grew so thick they looked like a black and green rug on a floor. Aunt Sis didn't really pick anymore, but she still insisted on being in the patch. After Mendy had filled both baskets and turned her fingertips purple, she helped Aunt Sis back to the porch.

Mendy settled Aunt Sis in a rocking chair on the porch and went inside. She dipped a cool drink of well water from the metal bucket in the kitchen and brought it out to her. "Here, Aunt Sis. You drink the water and sit a while. I'll be back in a little bit and take you inside." Mendy gave Aunt Sis's wrinkled hand a little squeeze and headed off to the Taj Mahal.

At the edge of Mr. Connor's woods, Mendy paused. Was it possible that the trespasser was Jeb Connor himself? *Well, even if it were, so what? He wouldn't really kill no person like they say,* Mendy told herself. *Leastways not a little girl.*

Besides, she could outrun old man Connor any day. And she'd promised to pay Mr. Hare a visit.

CHAPTER 3
TRESPASSERS

 hen Mendy arrived at the clearing, she stood very still and listened before stepping out into the open. She didn't hear anything, but she could see that someone had been there again. The remains of a fire made a black circle in the middle of the clearing. Beer bottles and crushed cigarette butts and cigars lay all around.

Mendy's heart raced. "Come on, baby," she said, picking up Mr. Hare, who was nibbling his favorite purple flowers. Now she knew there was more than one person trespassing in the Taj Mahal. She checked the branches of trees and bushes close by, looking for signs that this had been some kind of hunting party. This time of year, hunters could be after squirrels, groundhogs, coyotes, beavers, deer, or even black bears. But Mendy found no hunting traps or dog leavings, not even a dog track.

Mendy felt heartbroken as she looked around the

littered clearing. She stroked Mr. Hare as she thought. How dare people mess up the Taj Mahal like this? Whoever they were, they had no respect for the woods. Everyone knew you shouldn't carelessly set a fire in the middle of thick forest in the summer. Maybe teenagers had done this. Mendy had heard that sometimes they sneaked off doing things they had no business doing. Yes. That must be it.

Mendy squatted at the edge of the clearing. What could she do to stop them? She couldn't tell Mama or Daddy, because then they'd know she'd been in Jeb Connor's woods. It was up to her to handle the problem. Well, she would fix those kids if they came back.

Mendy put Mr. Hare on the ground and began to search for the trespassers' path. Like any good woodsman, she could read the telltale signs of broken twigs, torn leaves, footprints, and disturbed ground covering. By the footprints she found, Mendy judged there were four or five trespassers, all older boys or men.

Mendy's daddy had taught her a lot about tracking in the woods. And Grandma had told her about the honey traps her ancestor Great-Uncle Joe used to set. Mendy smiled grimly and set to work.

She marched off to the cave where she and Jeffrey hid their treasures and left supplies for their adventures in the woods—canned food, utensils, army blankets, tools, old clothes, and the long, sharp bowie knife that Daddy had given her as a gift. Mendy put on overalls and tied string around the pants legs. Then she cut off a piece of mosquito netting and stuck it in her pocket along with a pair of thick work gloves. Last, she picked up a large empty bucket.

Mendy returned to the clearing. She quickly carved a makeshift shovel from a fallen tree branch with her bowie knife and dug a deep hole near the trespassers' path. Then she set back out—but not before she ordered Mr. Hare back into the clearing. She never wanted him following her too far into the woods.

The great thing about having your own forest is that you know where everything is, and in this case Mendy knew the exact hollow tree where the honeybees lived. Now the trick was removing the beehive and placing it in the bucket. Her grandma had taught her about the "bee calm" bushes that grew on the north side of the woods. Mendy gathered leaves from the bushes and dropped them into a rusty tin can along with dry pine straw. Then she hurried back to the beehive and lit the contents of the tin can with a match. Standing upwind, Mendy fanned the smoke until it swirled around the tree and calmed the bees.

Mendy pulled the netting from her pocket and draped it over her head, tying a string around her neck to keep the netting in place. Then she slipped on her gloves. Mendy waited until all the buzzing stopped. Carefully she pulled out the honeycomb, making sure the queen was attached. A few bees buzzed softly near her head, but Mendy didn't move or swat at them. She knew they were not in the mood to attack.

Once the honeycomb was in the bucket, Mendy covered the top with mosquito netting, carried the bucket quickly to the hole she had dug, and set the honeycomb inside.

Her trap was nearly finished. The only thing left was to find some bait to lure the trespassers to it. The bait had to be something valuable—something boys or men would notice right away. What?

Mendy glanced at her bowie knife. Leaving it would mean she might never get it back. The knife meant a lot to her, but it was the only thing she could think of to use. Any boy worth his salt would recognize the hilt of a bowie knife. And he'd stop and pick it up, too.

Mendy found a thick piece of wood and plunged the knife into it as hard as she could. Then she tried to pull the knife out, but it stuck fast. Perfect. She set the wood and the knife into the hole alongside the honeycomb, arranging the mosquito netting around it. Then she covered the hole with grass and leaves until only the hilt of the knife was sticking out. Now her trap was ready. She hoped that whoever came along would get curious about the knife, pull it out, and release the whole swarm of bees.

She almost laughed thinking about the surprise those kids were in for. She figured they'd be scared off the minute the buzzing began, and she hoped they'd never come back. Mendy wasn't worried that setting the trap was wrong, either. If the trespassers got stung, it would just serve them right for messing up the Taj Mahal.

Mendy was just taking off her work gloves when she felt a thump on her backside. She swung around, swatting her hand at her back. Then she saw Mr. Hare, sitting still, watching, nose twitching. "Hello, Mr. Hare. What you doing, jumping on my back like that?" She knelt down so he could hop into her lap. Mendy held him with both hands. "You've grown too big to sit in the palm of one hand, my little friend," she said, smiling. She cuddled him and then set him back down. "I've got to go now. You be good."

Mendy started out of the clearing. From the corner of her eye, she spotted Mr. Hare hopping over to the trap. Mendy stopped to see what he was going to do. She hoped he wouldn't start messing with the trap. He didn't. She watched as Mr. Hare lay down near the trap, his nose twitching in the air. Mendy wished she hadn't set the trap so close to his purple flowers. But it was too late now. She waved good-bye, glad that he didn't try to follow her.

She found Aunt Sis asleep on the porch, sitting straight up in the wooden rocker. Mendy woke her up and helped her inside. "I'll be back as soon as I can," Mendy said. "To help you with your . . ." What? Mendy needed an excuse to come back, but she couldn't think of a thing.

"To help me with my watermelon patch," Aunt Sis said. "You gotta help me with my patch. Tell your mama that."

Mendy looked at Aunt Sis. Did the old woman understand that she was coming in part to go into the forest?
Mendy shook her head. No. Probably not, but the watermelon excuse would be great. Mendy got her blackberries
and headed home.

That night Mendy realized how quiet the house was
without her brothers and sisters. She even missed Morris
correcting everyone's English. And Daddy—she missed
Daddy most of all.

Mendy fell asleep thinking about her trap in the forest
but woke up sweating from a dream. In her dream, piano
notes were chasing her through the woods.

The next day Mendy got up early and did her chores.
Then she asked if she could go help Aunt Sis with her
watermelon patch.

When Mendy got to the cabin, Aunt Sis was outside
making soap in a black kettle. It was one of her bad days.
"You old coot. Get on away from here. Ma—Ma, come
and get Bo. He's messing with me while I make the soap."

"Aunt Sis, it's me, Mendy. Your mama ain't here no
more," Mendy said gently.

"Bo, get on away. I'm gonna hit you with this stick.
Get. I will kill you if you don't get away from them
chickens," Aunt Sis said, snatching up her walking stick.

She raised it to strike at Mendy.

"I'll be back later," Mendy said, backing up. She hated it when Aunt Sis acted mean. It seemed like if you weren't mean when you were in your right mind, you wouldn't be mean out of it. "I'll help you when I get back," Mendy said. Then, trying to sound like a grown woman, she added, "Now don't get burned messing with that fire." Mendy hoped the warning would help Aunt Sis be careful, even if she wasn't in her right mind.

Mendy headed for the woods. When she neared the clearing, she slowed down and approached quietly, peeping around the trees until she was sure no one else was around. She ran to check the honey trap. Even from a ways away, she could see the hilt of the bowie knife sticking up, just the way she'd left it. It seemed the trespassers hadn't come back.

Then Mendy stopped short. A few feet from the hole lay fragments of honeycomb. Someone had torn the trap apart. *Mr. Hare couldn't have done this,* Mendy thought. *Could it have been a bear looking for honey?* Mendy stood up and looked for tracks. Bear tracks looked like little fat baby feet. But there weren't any bear tracks. In fact, there were *no* tracks, none at all. Someone had deliberately swept them away.

Where was Mr. Hare? "Mr. Hare," she called, making a purring sound so he'd come to her. He didn't hop out.

Mendy squatted down, eyeing the remnants. She saw

no sign of dead bees. That meant that whoever had disturbed the trap knew about bees and had removed the honeycomb without getting stung.

Mendy sat down on the tree stump. She shook her leg while she thought. Why had the trespassers put the bowie knife back in the same exact spot and covered the trap with grass and sticks again? Her stomach did a little flip. Maybe they were reversing the trap.

Mendy got up slowly. She sniffed the air. It stank pretty badly. It wasn't the smell of a skunk, though. Mendy knew their smell well. She and Grandma used to trap skunks to get the healing oils from them.

She sniffed again. What *was* that awful smell? Mendy walked over to the trap and kicked the grass and sticks away. Honey stuck to her shoe. She could see something dark and crusted on the hilt of the bowie knife now as it stuck up out of the earth. Mendy knelt down. It looked like dried blood.

Someone was messing with her—trying to scare her. Those teenagers had probably mixed molasses with catsup, she told herself. She and Jeffrey had done the same thing to pretend they were wounded in battle. Had *Jeffrey* found the trap and left her a surprise inside? They often played tricks on each other—but he wouldn't play like this when he knew she was mad. No, she was sure it wasn't Jeffrey.

Mendy didn't want to get the mess on her hands. She spotted a ripped piece of white cloth that the trespassers must have left behind. Mendy palmed the cloth and grasped the handle of the bowie knife. Her muscles bulged as she pulled, but the knife didn't come up. Had they left the knife inside the chunk of wood? She pulled again, harder this time. Dirt and leaves fell away as the bundle lifted. The knife pulled free, and the bundle fell back to the ground. A soft tuft of fur escaped and floated away. In that split second, Mendy knew what the bundle was. Mr. Hare had been killed.

Mendy snatched her hand away, and the knife clumped back down on top of the bundle. Mendy's tears spilled down her cheeks, past her lips and her chin, and dropped silently to the ground while she rocked on her knees. No responsible hunter would kill a tame animal. Never. Anyone could tell this rabbit was tame.

Mendy pivoted quickly, gazing around the Taj Mahal. Were the trespassers still here, watching her? No, she would have known if anyone was around.

Even if they were, Mendy didn't care. She would bury Mr. Hare before she left, no matter who was here. Mendy wiped her eyes dry. Now she was more mad than sad. She got a blanket from her and Jeffrey's cave—no, *her* cave— and came back. Mr. Hare was wrapped in a dingy white cloth with some strange reddish symbol painted on it. Whoever did this was sending her a message—they wanted her to be afraid. Well, too bad. She wouldn't let them scare her off.

Mendy closed her eyes and took a deep breath to stop her trembling. With a stick, she gently nudged the soiled cloth from Mr. Hare's small, stiff body. She shoved the cloth around so that she could see what was on it. It was a red circle with a cross inside it. She'd never seen that mark before, but now it was stamped in her mind.

Salty tears dropped from Mendy's eyes as she wrapped Mr. Hare securely inside the blanket. Mendy found her makeshift shovel and dug a hole, hidden a few feet away in the low-lying brush. She knew people got buried six feet under the ground, but she couldn't dig that far by herself. *If Jeffrey was here* . . . She didn't want to think about that traitor. But as she dug she realized she needed help. Whoever was coming on her land was really evil. Her body was shaking badly. *Evil.* Until this happened, Mendy hadn't really known what evil was.

She had to do something. Maybe she could tell Daddy and Mama. Sure, and get a whipping for being out here in the first place. What about Aunt Sis? But what could Aunt Sis do to help? No, Mendy was on her own. Whoever had killed Mr. Hare needed to be taught a lesson, and Mendy vowed to do just that.

Mendy picked a few wildflowers, the purple ones that were Mr. Hare's favorite, and placed them on top of the blanket. She put him in the earth and covered him up as best she could. Then she stood over him and recited what she thought she'd heard preachers say: "Ashes to ashes, dust to dust, I'm so glad you came to live with us."

She found a few large rocks and placed them over Mr. Hare's grave to protect it. She made a cross of two sticks tied together with long leaves. Then Mendy lay down beside Mr. Hare's grave and cried until she fell into an exhausted sleep.

When she woke up it was almost dark. Mama would give her a whipping for sure. Mendy stopped only a second to stare at her bowie knife lying near the grave. No, it was no longer hers. The knife belonged to evil now. She didn't want it.

Mendy didn't even stop back at Aunt Sis's. She just walked home, wishing she'd never made friends with Mr. Hare. If she'd left him alone after he was well again, like Daddy had said to, he might still be alive.

Mendy took her whipping for being late and went to bed. That night she dreamed about blood and ghosts. She woke up once, crying out so loud that Mama came to check on her.

Finally, Mendy turned on the lamp, opened her scrapbook, and stared at the picture of the Taj Mahal in India, trying to transport herself there. After a while, she flipped through the scrapbook and searched for a certain page until she found it.

Grandma had written one of Mrs. Roosevelt's sayings at the bottom of this page:

The more we dwell on our happy memories, the better it will be for us all.
My Day, May 18, 1943

Mendy turned off the light and lay on her back, looking up at the mattress of the top bunk. Tears seeped down her face as she recalled how, shortly after Mr. Hare came to her, she had started counting rabbits instead of sheep in order to fall asleep. But now Mendy couldn't sleep. It was plain as day that Mr. Hare had been killed because of her. She was the one who had tamed the poor rabbit and taught him to stay in the Taj Mahal. Of course, the people who killed Mr. Hare didn't know he belonged to Mendy, but maybe they had realized he must belong to whoever set the trap. And they were trying to send a message to that person: *Stay away.* Yes, she was the reason Mr. Hare was dead. They had killed Mr. Hare just to make a point. What a shame. Mendy squeezed her eyes shut and tried hard to remember Mr. Hare happily nibbling flowers.

As Mendy drifted off to sleep, she had another memory. Once Grandma took her along to a birthing, and she let Mendy see the baby right after it was born. The baby was all yellow-looking, and his eyelids were stuck together.

The baby was so still he didn't even twitch. Mendy didn't think he was even breathing. Grandma spit on her hands and rubbed the baby's eyes. Then she took some dust from a pouch around her neck and placed it in her own mouth. When Grandma removed it from her mouth, it was a little lump no bigger than a pea. Grandma gently pushed the pea shape into the baby's mouth. A few seconds later, Mendy could see his color change back to normal brown. And then, just like that, the baby opened his eyes and started kicking and crying. Everybody said it was a miracle from God. Grandma said, "It weren't no miracle, just God doing what he do every single day."

Mendy remembered Grandma talking to the mother a few months later, when the baby died. She had said the same words then: "God just doing what he do every single day. Be grateful your baby come to know you."

Mendy switched the lamp back on and wrote under Mrs. Roosevelt's quote: *I can be thankful that Mr. Hare came to know me.* Then Mendy prayed, "God bless Mama, Daddy, my sisters and brothers, Grandma, Aunt Sis, Mrs. Roosevelt, Mr. Hare, and everybody. Amen."

Chapter 4
Daddy's News

Mendy woke to the smell and sound of bacon sizzling in the kitchen. Daddy must be home! Whenever Daddy had been off working, Mama cooked him bacon and eggs for breakfast.

Mendy washed up and dressed quickly. Seeing Daddy was probably the only thing that could cheer her up today.

As Mendy walked into the kitchen, Mama was saying to Daddy, "I don't want you to take Mendy over there. One day there's gonna be trouble with a capital *T* over there."

Mendy wanted to say, *Is that the only letter you know, Mama?* But instead she said, "Where is it you don't want Daddy to take me?"

"Nowhere," Mama said abruptly. "Sit down and eat your breakfast."

Daddy cleared his throat. "I was going to take you

to the Highlander School today, that's all. I was thinking you could go swimming in the pond while I take care of a plumbing job."

"Oh, boy!" Mendy shouted.

Mama glared at Daddy. "What did I just tell you 'bout this, Ben?"

"It'll be okay, Olivia," Daddy said. "Those people over at the Highlander care about colored folk. They ain't just talking about it—they are living it."

Mendy wanted to ask Daddy what he meant by that, but Mama spoke first.

"Mendy, go outside," she said, biting her top lip.

"Outside? I haven't eaten my breakfast yet, Mama."

"Forget it," Daddy said. "Eat your breakfast, Mendy. You can still go with me. You just don't have to swim, that's all. Myles Horton likes for you to visit Highlander." Mr. Horton was the founder and president of Highlander. "He's always bragging how you practically spent the summer over there with me last year and explored every last inch of the grounds."

Mama slammed the frying pan down on the stove. "Ben, I don't want her going there, period. Somebody's gonna get hurt over there one day."

"Well, maybe somebody *will* get hurt. It's better to get hurt fighting for what's right than stay safe doing nothing."

"Who's fighting, Daddy?" Mendy asked, looking from her mama to her daddy.

"See?" Mama said, shaking her head. "Don't go putting that foolishness into her head. I never should have let you take her over there in the first place."

Daddy said, "Myles Horton is the only white man in Grundy County who'd hire me to do his plumbing. We ought to support his cause. It's our cause, too."

Mendy saw Mama take a deep breath and put her palms down on the edge of the stove. Nobody knew grandma's saying, "You can catch more flies with honey than you can with stink," better than Mama. Mama said slow and soft, "I want her to practice piano today—honey. So why don't you take her fishing this evening?"

Mendy sighed. Whenever Mama talked softly and called Daddy "honey," that was the end of it. He caved in.

"All right, all right. I won't take her to Highlander. But now, that 'honey' sounded awful sweet, baby. Why don't you give me a little kiss?" Daddy said, pointing to his cheek.

Mama pecked Daddy on the cheek and hugged his head to her.

Then, thankfully, Mendy saw Li'l Ben coming into the kitchen rubbing his eyes with the back of his hand, saying, "I'm hungry, Mama."

Mama giggled and said, "Okay, baby," looking straight at Daddy.

Mendy didn't see what was so funny. She put jelly on her last biscuit, wrapped it in a napkin, and walked outside. Just as the screen door slammed shut, she heard her mama say, "Don't go disappearing, Mendy. You gotta practice the piano this morning."

Mendy waited on the step until Daddy came out, heading for his truck.

"Daddy, can I go with you now?" she asked him. "To Highlander?"

He sat down beside her. "You know you can't go. You heard your mama. I'll take you fishing this evening instead."

"Why does Mama not want me at Highlander?" she asked, accepting that he was on Mama's side now.

"Oh, that. Don't tell your mama I told you this, okay?"

Mendy nodded.

"The Highlander School fights for the rights of all people, Mendy—white and colored. Do you understand? Some people don't like that."

Mendy frowned up. "Is something bad happening at Highlander?"

"Of course it ain't. But your mama thinks something might go wrong, since some folks ain't happy with Myles Horton's beliefs."

"Who ain't happy with his beliefs?"

"Plenty of people, Wild Trapper."

"But Mr. Horton is the nicest man, Daddy. And he's your good friend," Mendy said, dropping her head. She wanted to tell Daddy right then about the people in the woods. *Probably some people are just plain mean,* she thought. *They ain't got no reason for disliking Mr. Horton, the same as whoever hurt Mr. Hare ain't got no reason.* But just then, Mama came and stood in the doorway.

"I hear what you saying out there, Ben. Don't you say another word. She don't need to know nothing 'bout them hateful white people. Let her be innocent a little longer, for goodness sake."

Mendy felt confused. What was Mama talking about? What hateful white people? Of course, Mendy knew that whites often treated coloreds different. In stores, white people got waited on before coloreds. Colored folk couldn't try on clothes or shoes; to get shoes the right size, they had to trace their feet on a paper bag. And when coloreds went to the movies they had to sit in what folk called the "buzzard roost," up in the balcony. Daddy said if you were nearsighted, you couldn't see a thing. What bothered Mendy most, though, was that the white kids had a big school with new books, while all the coloreds had was a one-room school and the white kids' hand-me-down books. She hated that white children had already written the answers in the books and put their names in ink where it says *This book belongs to.* But that's just how things were, Mendy thought. Surely Mama didn't mean hateful the way those people who hurt Mr. Hare were hateful. Did she? A chill raced through Mendy.

"Ben, you'd best get going," Mama said. "Come on inside, Mendy, I want to teach you a little ditty on the piano."

Mendy got up, grumbling all the way inside. She
plopped down on the piano bench and waited for
Mama. She let out a big sigh as she listened to Daddy
driving away.

Mama sat down beside Mendy. "There's some things
you don't have to learn about just yet. There's plenty
of time to know about the world. We're going to have
a good summer together, just you and me. How about
while Li'l Ben's playing with his logs, I'll teach you a song
my mama taught me when I was your age?"

Mendy frowned. *Here it comes, another church song.*
Mama began to sing:

> *There was a tree, the prettiest tree,*
> *The prettiest tree you ever did see.*
> *The tree in the ground*
> *And the green grass growing all around, all around,*
> *And the green grass growing all around.*

"Come on, sing it with me," Mama said to Mendy.

Mendy began to sing and play the tune on her piano
keys. Soon they were both laughing and playing and
singing and getting all the verses mixed up. Mendy forgot
that it was Mama—strict, stern Mama. This was fun.

When they finally stopped, both of them breathless,
grinning at each other, Mendy felt a flood of tears coming.
She started crying.

"What's the matter, baby?" Mama asked, pulling Mendy to her. "What you crying for?"

Mendy didn't answer. She just hugged Mama tightly and wished she could stay right there forever.

Mendy finished practicing the piano and hurried through her chores. After she was done brushing down Daddy's mare, Tandy, Mendy got a bucket and a small shovel and started digging up fat, juicy worms for bait. She wanted to be ready when Daddy came back. Mendy got their fishing poles and put them on the porch. Then she went in to ask Mama to fix a picnic basket. But Mama was way ahead of her. The basket was already waiting on the counter.

Mendy sat on the porch, just looking for pictures in the shapes of the clouds and trying to recall only good memories about Mr. Hare, until Daddy came back. When Mendy jumped in Daddy's truck, Mama's last words were, "Mendy, don't be running wild. And mind your manners."

As they drove along the mountain roads, Daddy told stories about mountain trappers and Great-Uncle Joe and the days when Daddy was a boy. As the truck bumped along the dirt and gravel road, Daddy's stories began to cheer Mendy up, despite her broken heart.

"Mendy, I used to have a spinning top whittled from

a pine knot. I loved that top. Then Grandpa Ben made me a goose-quill whistle and I thought I'd blow my fool head off. But my favorite of all was the popgun that my daddy made from a hollow cane. Why, I could hit almost anything with that gun. Wild Trapper, did I ever tell you about the time I shot a buzzard with it? Your grandma like to had a fit. She never wanted me to hunt just for sport. She always said, if you kill an animal, you got to ask it for forgiveness, and you better be using it for something like food, clothing, shelter, or in her case, medicine. You know how your grandma was."

"Daddy, do you think a person who kills a rabbit just to get back at someone is mean?"

Her daddy looked over at her, raising his eyebrows. "Naw, they ain't just mean—they're crazy. Who killed a rabbit to get back at someone?"

"Nobody, I was just asking," Mendy said. *Crazy.* The word rumbled around in her head.

"Mendy. You ain't in no trouble, are you?" her daddy asked, breaking into her thoughts.

She shook her head no.

"Oh, I almost forgot," Daddy said. "I got some big news for you. Somebody special is coming to Highlander real soon."

"Who, Daddy? Who?" Mendy asked, her excitement rising. "Who's coming to Highlander?"

"Are you ready for this?"

"Daddy," Mendy whined. "Please stop playing and tell me."

"Somebody your grandma would have loved to meet."

A huge grin popped on Mendy's face. Now Mendy had an idea who was coming. "You kidding me, Daddy?"

"Nope. Got the flyer right here," Daddy said, taking a folded paper out of his shirt pocket and passing it to Mendy.

Mendy screamed with delight. Mrs. Eleanor Roosevelt would be at Highlander on June 17. That was less than two weeks away. She was speaking to encourage good race relations. Mendy couldn't believe it—Mrs. Anna Eleanor Roosevelt right there in Monteagle, Tennessee, on Tuesday, June 17, 1958.

"Can we go, Daddy? To hear her?"

"I'm thinking on it, Wild Trapper. I'm thinking on it hard," Daddy said. "Now just calm down and don't say nothing to anyone about it, especially your mama. Just let me think on a plan."

"You remember what you told me about the man you knew in the war, Daddy?" Mendy asked.

"Sure I do."

"Tell me again," Mendy said. "I like hearing that story."

Her daddy smiled. "Well, all right. You know I was stationed all the way over in a place called Brisbane, Australia. It was 1943 and I was friends with a man named . . ."

"Calvin Johnson," Mendy said, grinning.

"That's right," Daddy said. "You got a good memory. Back then, the army still had a white division and a colored division. Why, even the Red Cross was segregated. But we could all be in the canteen—remember, that's like a small café—at the same time. Now, one day we're sitting in the canteen, me and Calvin, when this tall white woman comes walking in."

"And you whispered to Mr. Johnson, 'Man, that's Eleanor Roosevelt.' And neither one of you could believe it."

"Yep. And about that time, she walks behind the counter and begins shaking the men's hands until she come to me and Calvin, the only two colored men sitting in there. Calvin was eating an ice cream cone.

"He put that cone in his left hand so he could shake her hand. He told her he was from Pittsburgh and she smiled and said, 'What do you know, we have a Yankee here.' And all the soldiers started cheering and laughing. Then Mrs. Roosevelt looked Calvin straight in the eye and said . . ."

"'May I have some of that ice cream?' And you and Mr. Johnson couldn't hardly believe it," Mendy said.

"Yep. And then Mrs. Roosevelt gently took the cone from Calvin's hand, took a bite, and handed it back to him. And she said, 'You see? That didn't hurt at all, did it? You won't even miss it.'

"Them white boys was red as beets. I bet not one of them ever thought he'd live to see a white lady eat a colored person's food. No sirree. Why, that room was so quiet you coulda heard a mouse peeing on cotton. When she got to me, I was so nervous I couldn't even lift my hand for her to shake it. So she lifted it up for me. After that, me and Calvin always said Mrs. Eleanor Roosevelt was . . ."

"I know," Mendy said. "The nicest white woman you'd ever met. And now it's my time to see her."

"I'm thinking on it, Wild Trapper. Just be patient."

Mendy settled back in her seat. Her face lit up like a Christmas tree as she reread the flyer. Wow. Eleanor Roosevelt was coming to Monteagle, Tennessee!

Daddy started singing:

> *Heavenly shades of night are falling*
> *It's twilight time*
> *Out of the mist your voice is calling*
> *It's twilight time*
> *When purple-colored curtains*
> *Mark the end of day*
> *I hear you, my dear, at twilight time*

Mendy said, "That's a pretty song, Daddy. What's the name of it?"

"'Twilight Time' by The Platters. You're right, it sure is pretty. Not as pretty as my daughter Mendy, though. Nope. Ain't no song prettier than my Mendy," Daddy said, grinning.

Mendy grinned too. She felt happier than she had for days, since she'd first spotted the cigar. "I hope we catch the biggest widemouth bass that's ever been caught in these parts, Daddy."

"Me too, Mendy. Me too."

That night Mendy felt so excited about Mrs. Roosevelt coming to Tennessee, she thought she'd burst wide open. She just hoped Daddy could come up with something really convincing so that Mama would let Mendy go to the Highlander School on June 17.

The next morning, after Daddy left for work, Mendy did all her chores cheerfully. After lunch she didn't even complain about taking Li'l Ben outside to play before his nap. Then Mendy offered to string beans for Mama.

As Mendy sat on the porch alone and worked on the beans, she forced herself to think of what had happened to poor Mr. Hare. She had promised herself she'd teach those mean people a lesson. She was scared to go back to the clearing, but Daddy always said, "Just because you afraid don't mean you can't do something. It just means you need to be more careful about doing it, is all."

CHAPTER 5

THE PERFECT PLAN

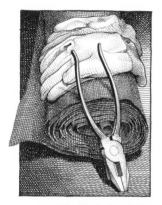

Mendy finished stringing the beans, then waited for a good moment to ask Mama if she could go visit Aunt Sis. Her chance came when she caught sight of Mama out in the yard, talking to one of the ladies from church. Mama seemed sad that Mendy didn't want to stay with her, but she said all right. Mama didn't even make Mendy practice the piano before she left.

Mendy scrounged around in the barn until she found some old work gloves, some leftover wire screening, and wire cutters. She packed them in a burlap sack and put it in her wagon. This time she'd set a better trap.

When Mendy arrived at Aunt Sis's house, there was no sign of her. Mendy stood on the porch and called, "Aunt Sis. Aunt Sis, where are you?" but there was no answer. Where could she be this late in the afternoon? She hardly ever left home. The rolling store even brought her groceries out. This was a horse-drawn wagon with a colored man driving it and a white man working in the back, taking grocery orders and seeing to the money. The rolling store didn't usually serve coloreds, but the white family in Sewanee that Aunt Sis used to work for made sure it stopped at her cabin each week.

Mendy looked under the crabapple tree near the edge of the woods. Sometimes on warm afternoons, Aunt Sis sat under the tree fanning herself. She never seemed to notice the apples dropping like rifle bullets all around her. Mendy hated to sit under the tree with her, since you might get clunked in the head at any moment.

Mendy walked back up to the porch. Maybe Aunt Sis was sick. The screen door wasn't latched, so Mendy went inside. Aunt Sis wasn't there, but everything looked in place; the bed was made up and the kitchen was clean. Aunt Sis might be "bad to forget" and often confused, but she still kept her house clean—so clean you could eat off her floor. Then Mendy noticed that Aunt Sis's walking stick was gone. Aunt Sis took her stick everywhere she went. Mendy decided maybe someone had come and picked her up to take her into town. Lots of folk who were raised in the mountains and hollows didn't lock up when they left home.

Mendy took her wagon and headed into the woods. She needed to set her trap and get back home before Mama came looking to see what she was up to.

When Mendy reached the clearing, she let out her breath with relief. There was no sign that the trespassers had been back. Mendy checked the low brush to make sure that Mr. Hare's grave hadn't been disturbed. The makeshift cross still stood guard.

Mendy walked back into the clearing and emptied the contents of her wagon. Then she picked up an empty sack and got to work.

Creeks and streams speckled the woods of the Cumberland Plateau. Mendy searched the damp edge of the nearest creek until she found what she was looking for—a nest of water snakes. The snakes were lying curled up under a rock, sluggish from the cool darkness. Grandma had taught Mendy how to catch snakes. Mendy could even catch a rattler with her bare hands and milk the fangs for the venom, which Grandma used to treat folks for snake-bites. Catching these harmless water snakes wouldn't even be scary.

Mendy moved around the nest quietly, careful not to step on a twig that might snap or leaves that might crunch. Suddenly she pounced, letting the sack land right on top of the nest of snakes. She snatched them up into the sack and tied it off just like Grandma had taught her.

Mendy dragged the sack over to the hole where she'd set the honey trap. She planned to set her new trap in the same hole, then make the spot look exactly the way the trespassers had left it when they reversed her trap. She

knew they would be back to check it. Every hunter came
back to check his traps.

Mendy carefully emptied the sackful of snakes into
the hole and secured the wire screening over them. Then
she spotted the blood-stained rag that the trespassers
had wrapped around Mr. Hare, still lying in the same place
she'd left it. She pulled on her work gloves, took a deep
breath, and picked up the cloth between the tips of her
fingers. She could see the red circle and the cross. Mendy
wrapped the cloth around grass and leaves until it was
about the same size as Mr. Hare. She placed the bundle
on top of the screening. Below it, she could see the snakes
writhing against the mesh already.

Now came the hardest part: picking up the bowie
knife. Mendy had thought she'd never touch the knife
again. She dreaded touching it now. But it had to be done.
Unless the hilt of that knife was sticking out of the trap
just like before, the trespassers would know she had been
back. Mendy stuck the knife into the wire mesh. Then she
put grass and leaves around the knife's hilt. The minute
one of the trespassers lifted the knife to see if Mr. Hare
was still there, the wire would come up, too.

A snakebite would be a hard lesson. These were plain
water snakes but they looked like copperheads, the most
poisonous snakes around. Whoever got bit would spend
some anxious hours fearing for his life.

Mendy started packing up, then hesitated. Was it right

to leave this trap for the trespassers? Her mind went back to the last time she ever saw Mr. Hare. *They killed an innocent rabbit. You darn tootin' it's right,* she decided.

She stopped by the cave to see if maybe Jeffrey had come by. But there was no sign he'd been there. She felt angry that Jeffrey had just accepted that they couldn't be friends anymore. It hurt that he could give up so easily.

Mendy took out the secret treasures they kept in the cave to signify they'd be blood sister and brother forever— quartz crystals, agate, a piece of sparkly green fluorite, yellow sandstone banded with delicate brown lines, even the skeletal remains of a box turtle who might have lived for sixty years. Mendy took it all to the edge of the stream to throw it away. This was the end of the pact between her and chicken Jeffrey.

Then Mendy saw it—an Eastern painted turtle shading on a nearby rock. Its beautiful head and shell were patterned with every color in the mountains. Mendy had heard tell of these turtles, but she'd never come face-to-face with one. She took it as a sign. Grandma said you should never ignore the signs. Mendy wrapped the treasures back up and returned them to the cave. Then she pulled the wagon back toward Aunt Sis's house.

As Mendy walked, she noticed how dark it was under the trees' thick canopy. Was night coming already? Had it taken her that long to find the snakes? Maybe. She couldn't use the sky to tell time in the thickest part of the woods. Mendy began walking a little faster.

She stopped abruptly. She had heard something—a sound like a baby's whimpering. Mendy followed the sound. She had to stop every few feet, because the sound was so faint and her rusty wagon so loud. She heard the whimpering more clearly now. Mendy ran toward the sound, leaving the wagon behind. Suppose a child or an animal had gotten hurt or trapped somewhere? The forest was full of sinkholes and caves.

Mendy cocked her head to listen. The sound was coming from her right. She knew there was a cave and an old well off in that direction. Folks said a mountain man used to live there. Mendy took a few steps forward, but she halted as she caught sight of something half-hidden in the leaves. She put out a toe and nudged it. It was a stick—Aunt Sis's walking stick.

Mendy picked it up, her heart racing. She followed the whimpering sound to the entrance of the cave. "Aunt Sis," she called. "You in there? Aunt Sis, answer me."

Mendy could hear the sound more clearly now. It was Aunt Sis, talking and whimpering at the same time.

On hands and knees, Mendy peered inside the cave, but she could see only darkness. "Aunt Sis, what you doing in there? Please, it's me, Mendy. Come on out now."

Aunt Sis ain't never been this bad before. I should go get help, Mendy thought. But was there time to fetch somebody and get back before darkness fell?

"Aunt Sis, I'm coming to get you," Mendy said. "Just sit still." She went back to the wagon and grabbed a flashlight. She crawled into the dark cave, struggling to hold the wavery beam of light steady. The cave floor felt cold and damp. Mendy's hand squished a bug. But she kept crawling until she reached Aunt Sis. Mendy held her flashlight so that she could see Aunt Sis and Aunt Sis could see her.

Aunt Sis cowered against the back wall of the cave, clutching a white cloth. In the flashlight's beam, Mendy could see that the cloth had a red marking on it. Mendy's heart hurt.

"Aunt Sis, what are you doing in here? Where did you get that cloth?" Mendy said while trying to snatch it from her.

Had Aunt Sis killed the poor rabbit? Mendy remembered her daddy saying that only a crazy person would have killed Mr. Hare. Didn't some people say Aunt Sis was crazy? What if Aunt Sis had killed Mr. Hare, thinking he was something else or not knowing what she was doing? Mendy tried to push the thought from her mind. No, Mendy wouldn't let herself think that.

"This here's mine," Aunt Sis said, pulling the cloth from Mendy's grip. "The Devil done come. This *proof* the Devil is here." Aunt Sis rocked back and forth.

Mendy tried to take Aunt Sis's hand to calm her, but she jerked it away. Even if Aunt Sis had killed the rabbit, Mendy knew now she couldn't be mad at her. It was clear

Aunt Sis was more confused than Mendy had thought possible.

"Y'all ain't gonna get us no more. No. No more wailing, no more beatings," Aunt Sis was saying now, almost singing like she was in church.

Mendy sat back on her heels. Her head brushed the top of the cave. How in the world had Aunt Sis gotten back in here? "Come on now, Aunt Sis. It's me, Mendy. Remember? I sit with you under the crabapple tree sometimes. Remember? Come on out with me." Mendy inched toward her.

Aunt Sis screamed so loud, Mendy put her hands up to her ears.

"All right, all right," Mendy said, thinking fast. "Listen, Aunt Sis, I'll take you out past the Devil. How about that? I won't let the Devil get you." She shined the flashlight so Aunt Sis could see her face clearly. "See? It's me, Mendy. I'll keep the Devil away from you, Aunt Sis. I promise."

But Aunt Sis shook her head. "The Devil ain't scared of you," she said.

Mendy almost laughed. Aunt Sis wasn't so crazy that she didn't know that much. If the Devil was out there, he sure wasn't scared of Mendy. Mendy sat down and moved as close as she could to Aunt Sis. She stroked Aunt Sis's wrinkled hand gently, on the verge of crying at how mad Mama and Daddy would be if she didn't get home soon. Then Mendy had another idea.

She started singing the ditty that Mama had taught her yesterday. If Mama's mama knew it, maybe Aunt Sis knew it, too. Mendy had been humming it ever since in her mind. Suddenly, Aunt Sis started singing it with Mendy. She squeezed Mendy's hand back. Mendy sang and pulled on Aunt Sis's hand until she finally led her out of the cave.

Now it *was* dark. The last trace of sunlight had vanished from the woods, and a chill had crept into the air.

Mendy removed the blanket that she kept as a lining in the wagon and wrapped it around Aunt Sis's shoulders. Gently, she took the white cloth from Aunt Sis's hand and stuck it into her own pocket. Then she helped Aunt Sis into the wagon and laid the walking stick across her lap. "You ready to go home?" Mendy asked, wishing she'd never started coming to these woods at all. Just like Mama said, these woods were trouble with a capital *T*.

It wasn't easy pulling Aunt Sis in the wagon over the ridges, rocks, and thistled brush. It took Mendy longer than she wanted it to take. Aunt Sis sang "The Green Grass Growing All Around" every step of the way.

Once they reached Aunt Sis's cabin, Mendy helped her wash up and gave her something to eat before putting her to bed. Mendy waited until she heard Aunt Sis snoring lightly. Then she pulled the cloth out of her pocket and examined it in the moonlight that shone through the window.

As she stared at the red mark on the cloth, Mendy's

hand began to shake. The cloth was painted with that strangely shaped cross inside a circle—the same symbol she'd seen on the dingy cloth Mr. Hare had been wrapped in. Could Aunt Sis really have killed Mr. Hare?

Mendy listened as the trill of the singing toad echoed in the trees just like a song, the way it always did on warm summer nights. It was late now, which meant Mendy was in for another whipping. She looked down at her clothes; they were full of dirt and ripped in places. Her legs were scratched up, too. Mama and Daddy both might whip her this time. Mendy checked that Aunt Sis was sleeping peacefully. Then she took the wagon and went home.

On the way, Mendy thought about Aunt Sis. Her sleeping face had looked as sweet as a baby's. No, Aunt Sis wouldn't have killed Mr. Hare. Besides, Aunt Sis wasn't the person who left the mushy-topped cigar or the beer bottles and cigarette butts in the clearing.

But if Aunt Sis didn't kill Mr. Hare, then who did? And why was Aunt Sis holding a cloth marked just like the one Mr. Hare was wrapped in? Maybe she had just found the cloth in the woods. But then, what did the red mark mean? Was *that* what had made Aunt Sis so scared?

Mendy recalled Aunt Sis clutching the cloth and babbling, "The Devil done come . . . This *proof* the Devil is here." What had Aunt Sis meant by that? Mendy shivered. She herself had surely felt the Devil's presence in the clearing. Now, thinking of the evil people who killed

Mr. Hare, Mendy considered something else. What if the trespassers knew about Aunt Sis's cabin, not far from the clearing? What if they had come to her house to hurt her, and that's why she ran to the cave to hide?

Mendy felt sure now that the trespassers weren't just stupid kids. Aunt Sis wouldn't have been frightened like that by any kids. These were men, and whoever they were, Mendy felt certain they were dangerous, not just to animals but to people. She needed to stop them before they did something worse to Aunt Sis. Mendy felt weak with relief when her house came into view. She took her whipping without protest.

Mendy wished she could just tell Daddy everything that had happened. He might know what could have scared Aunt Sis enough to send her to the cave, or what the symbol on the cloth meant. But tonight, even Daddy was mad at her.

Mendy went to bed, but she tossed and turned, unable to sleep. What she had seen tonight made no sense to her. And uneasiness about the trap she had set began to creep over her. Maybe she should just leave these evil people alone. And besides, what she'd done with the snakes was mean and nasty. Sure, they were only water snakes, but whoever found them would think they were copperheads. Was it right to do that to a human for killing a rabbit, even if the rabbit was Mr. Hare? As Mendy lay there, she wished she knew whether she was doing the right thing.

But she had to do something to scare the men away in order to protect Aunt Sis.

And then the answer struck her: Doing something wrong will never set anything right. Isn't that what her parents and Grandma had taught her?

Tomorrow she would undo the trap. She'd just have to think of another way to protect Aunt Sis.

The next day was Saturday, so Mendy had fewer chores. She hurried to Aunt Sis's and was glad to see her back to her right mind. Aunt Sis greeted Mendy cheerful as ever.

"I got you an orange doper in yonder," Aunt Sis said. "Hit ain't cold but it's good." Aunt Sis would often say *hit* for *it*.

Mendy went inside and got the orange soda off the table. Grandma called them dopers, too. Mendy debated whether she should bring up Mr. Hare or the cave, but Aunt Sis seemed so peaceful that Mendy decided against it.

When Mendy went back out to the porch, Aunt Sis was standing and looking out at the dark clouds building up over the woods. "Hit's gon' be a frog strangler coming up in a few. We's best get on inside."

A few minutes later, hard rains thundered through the forest. The rain on the tin roof sounded like men buck dancing on top of the house. Aunt Sis whiled away the time telling Mendy stories about Grandma when she was a girl. Aunt Sis said that even when Mendy's grandma was little, she could heal animals and people.

"Your grandma was a pistol, though. She had a pet skunk. And when anybody bothered your grandma, naw, she weren't no fighter—she'd just let the skunk take it up for her. Ain't many folk wanna bother your grandma, neither."

Mendy laughed so hard that tears came to her eyes. It had been a long time since she'd laughed out loud.

Soon the rain stopped, and the sun came out and dried up the leaves quick as nothing. Mendy told Aunt Sis she'd be back later. Aunt Sis didn't realize it, but she'd given Mendy an idea.

Mendy headed to the Taj Mahal with a new plan. The snake trap would only have been good for revenge, but it wouldn't protect Aunt Sis or tell her who the men were. Aunt Sis's story had helped her figure out a trap to do just that.

At the clearing, Mendy undid the snake trap. Then she picked some herbs in the damp shade—catnip, quinine, and a red flower that Grandma said Mendy should not use "because it would knock a body out." Mendy stopped by her cave and got a sack, then went tracking, reading the forest floor as easily as she read her schoolbooks. The trees had protected the ground from the rain except for a light sprinkling.

Daddy had been teaching Mendy how to track since she was a little kid. Tracks with five toes on both front feet and hind feet meant coon, badger, skunk, beaver, porcupine, muskrat, or bear. Four toes on front and hind feet meant fox, wolf, coyote, bobcat, rabbit, even a house cat. If the paw print had small triangle marks in front of it from claws, that narrowed it down to a coon, skunk, coyote, fox, or dog.

Today Mendy was scouting for a critter with five toes in front and back, and triangle marks in front of the paws. She was looking for a white-striped skunk.

During the warm months, Mendy knew, skunks spent their days sleeping in thickets, so that's where she concentrated her search. Grandma always told her that even though skunks had sharp teeth and claws, they weren't attack animals. That's why they had spray. Grandma had showed her exactly how to approach a skunk to catch it. "If the skunk don't want no part of you, it's gonna show you it means business before it sprays. It'll raise its tail or stand on its hind legs, and as a last warning it'll stomp its front feet at you as if to say, *'Git!'*"

It didn't take Mendy long to find a skunk curled up asleep in a thicket. She tiptoed up to him and placed the herbs and the red flowers close to the thicket. Mendy hunkered down nearby and threw a stick toward the skunk. He raised up and stared in the direction of the thud. Then, almost like a gleeful child, he scurried over and sniffed the leaves and the red flowers that Mendy had left. Mendy watched the skunk eat until they were all gone. He took a few steps, then lay down. Mendy waited patiently until she could see he was sleeping soundly.

She carefully laid the skunk onto the sack. Then she loaded him in the wagon and headed back to the clearing. She put the skunk inside the hole along with a few twigs to eat and covered the top with the wire screen. When the skunk woke up, he could get out if he wanted to bad enough. Mendy didn't think the skunk would wake up tonight, though, and if he didn't, he'd likely sleep through the following day, too.

Mendy hoped the skunk would still be in the trap when the trespasser returned. The skunk would spray for sure if he were surprised down in the hole. Then the culprit would be easy to find, because he'd be full of skunk sulfur. Mendy put the red-marked cloth and the bowie knife back in place and smiled.

Mendy left the clearing feeling that this was the best plan yet. Nobody would get hurt, and she might actually learn who at least one of the trespassers was. Mendy stopped by to check on Aunt Sis and then headed home. Now Mendy felt more at peace. Soon she would know who'd been stirring up trouble at the Taj Mahal.

CHAPTER 6
TROUBLE WITH A CAPITAL *T*

The next day was Sunday, and Sunday was family day. Mendy knew there was no chance of slipping off to check her trap. She was sure the skunk would be sleeping anyway. He wouldn't attempt an escape until nighttime.

Mendy put on her Sunday dress, lace socks, and shoes without her usual arguments. After church, Daddy and Mama sat on the front porch, watching Mendy play with Li'l Ben in the front yard. A little later, Daddy churned ice cream while Mama made a peach cobbler for dinner. They ate dinner late.

Afterward, Daddy read to Mendy and Mama from a book that Myles Horton had sent home with him called *As a Man Thinketh*. Mama didn't say much, but Mendy could tell she would rather hear reading from the Bible. Mendy only half listened. Her thoughts kept going back to the trespassers. Had they come back to the clearing?

Had they found the skunk trap? Mendy bit back a grin, thinking about one of the trespassers getting sprayed. But then her stomach twisted. Maybe, she realized, he would think Aunt Sis had put the skunk down in the hole and go after her. Mendy needed to get to the Taj Mahal, but there just was no way to do it.

Finally, Daddy stopped reading and got ready to leave. He had to drive through the mountains to Chattanooga tonight for a blacksmithing job that was going to last all week. For the first time in her life, Mendy felt glad when she saw Daddy drive off.

The minute Mama went to bed, Mendy sneaked out. She saddled up Tandy, placed a canteen on the saddle, and rode toward the Taj Mahal.

As Mendy neared Jeb Connor's woods, she saw lights flickering among the thick trees like giant fireflies. A plume of smoke rose up from the clearing.

Heat flushed through Mendy's body. The people who had killed Mr. Hare and scared Aunt Sis were in the woods right now. Mendy felt her knees trembling. She hugged herself as a shiver traveled like a snake down her back.

At the edge of the woods, near the stream, she tied Tandy to a tree and removed the canteen. "I'll be back. Stay put," she whispered.

At the stream, she wet her feet and filled her canteen. Mendy moved silently through the woods, the way Daddy had taught her to sneak up on an animal.

Mendy began to hear sounds from the clearing—the noise of grown men talking and laughing. She stood very still and listened.

There seemed to be a lot of men, more than Mendy had expected. Snatches of words floated out to her—angry, mean words. She stood at attention, every muscle in her body tense. Her heart beat wildly inside her chest. Her palms itched with sweat. But she could not turn back now. She had to know who these people were.

Mendy knelt down, opened her canteen, and began to inch forward under the cover of thick thorn bushes. As she crawled, she held the canteen in front of her and soaked the leaf-covered ground with water to make her movements quieter. Thorns pricked her hands, knees, and arms. Tiny trickles of blood dotted her skin. Finally, she was close enough to peep through the tangle of bushes into the clearing.

What she saw stopped her breath.

A dozen men stood in a circle around a fire. White robes covered them from head to foot. They wore tall, pointed white hats. And they were waving white flags with that blood-red symbol.

Mendy shivered like a wet dog. In the flickering fire-light, the men looked like ghosts, or demons. Mendy was so close to the clearing that she could see a man's ring glint in the firelight, could see shoes scuffing the dirt. The men were shouting now, their jeering voices so loud that the sound pierced Mendy like arrows. She couldn't believe what she was hearing. The men were yelling about Myles Horton and the Highlander School. They were saying hateful things, calling Mr. Horton ugly names and saying he was a traitor. Mendy watched, her heart squeezed with pain as the men shouted and jeered. Tears streamed down her face. Why were they talking about Daddy's friend this way? Who were these men?

Mendy crawled backward until she was a safe distance away. Then she jumped up and ran, praying that the sound of her footsteps could not be heard. She shook so badly that she could barely untie Tandy from the tree. Mendy thought of Daddy saying people were upset with Myles Horton, and of Mama saying somebody would get hurt at Highlander one day. Would these men hurt Mr. Horton? Mendy couldn't just stand by and let that happen. And what about Aunt Sis? Suppose they did something else to her.

But what could Mendy do? She couldn't tell Mama she'd seen this. She wished Daddy were home. Who else could she tell?

Mendy's heart pounded loudly in her chest. She didn't know what to do, but she would do *something*. She had to.

When Mendy was safely back in her room, she went to the dresser that she shared with her sisters. She picked up the framed photo of Grandma that sat on top. Mendy held the picture frame tight and wished that Grandma were here. *She* would know what to do.

Mendy trembled in her bed all night. She could not sleep for thinking about what she'd seen in the woods. Mendy understood Mama better now. She understood what trouble with a capital *T* was, and it had something to do with that blood-red symbol. The symbol on the cloth that had been wrapped around Mr. Hare. The symbol on the cloth that Aunt Sis had clutched in her hand. The symbol on the flags those men waved in the air tonight.

Maybe Aunt Sis had been right after all. Maybe the Devil *was* here—in Jeb Connor's woods.

The next morning Mendy made a decision. There was only one person who could help her: Jeffrey. He was the only person she could talk to—or at least he was the only one who wouldn't whip her for going on Jeb Connor's land or punish her for sneaking out in the middle of the night. Mendy scribbled out a note in their secret code and hurried to Jeffrey's house.

The back yard looked deserted. Mendy slipped to the clothesline, set the note under a big gray rock that Jeffrey could see from his bedroom window, and turned the rock flat side up so Jeffrey would know she'd left a message. He'd be waiting for her at the spring right after lunch— unless he really was the chicken-livered dog that Mendy had seen that day with Mama.

After lunch, when Mama lay down to help Li'l Ben go
to sleep, Mendy sneaked out of the house and ran all the
way to the spring. The afternoon was so hot she felt like
she'd pass out by the time she got there. Mendy splashed
cool water on her face, then paced near the spring, watching for Jeffrey.

Finally she walked to the big willow and sat down
under it. It looked like Jeffrey wasn't coming. She couldn't
believe it. What could she do now?

Just then something hit her on the head. For a second,
she felt like she was sitting under Aunt Sis's crabapple
tree. She looked up but saw nothing. She snatched up a
willow twig and started picking her teeth with it.

Bop. A tiny rock bounced beside her.

"Hey, who's doing that?" Mendy yelled, jumping up.
"Don't hit me again or I'll—"

"Hey, Mend. Not so loud. It's me. Do you want me to
get caught?"

"You snot-nosed chicken! What do I care if you get
caught?"

"It won't be just me who'll get caught, Mend. And I
ain't no chicken, either."

"You're a chicken traitor, that's what you are."

"Is that why you put out the emergency code? To fuss
at me? Go on home, why don't you, and leave me be."

Mendy stopped. Jeffrey was it—the only one she
could talk to. "Naw, that ain't why I used the code. I'm in

trouble," she said, sitting back down under the tree.

"What type of trouble are you in?"

"I don't even know." Mendy sighed. "Bad trouble, though."

"Bad trouble that you don't know . . . How you know you're in trouble then?"

"Can you come down here, please?" Mendy said. "I'm tired of talking to a bird in a tree."

Jeffrey climbed down and sat beside her. "If we get caught again, I just want you to know my folks say they'll send me away to a boys' school."

"Come on, they wouldn't do that."

"I'm not so sure anymore. My pa's acting really strange lately. He wants to know where I am and who I'm with almost every minute."

"Well, I got bigger problems." Then she told him about finding the cigar and lighter in the Taj Mahal and what had happened to Mr. Hare. She told him about Aunt Sis hiding in the cave, and about the white-robed men in the woods shouting about Myles Horton. "You got any notions about all this?"

"It's the same thing," he said. "It's the same as about me and you."

"Me and you? What do you mean?"

"I mean those men are mad at Myles Horton because he lets whites and coloreds go to school together and do stuff together on his property. And . . . " Jeffrey hesitated, a red flush creeping up his face. "And, well, our folks don't want us together because whites and coloreds ain't supposed to be boyfriend and girlfriend."

"Boyfriend and girlfriend? We ain't no such thing. Who said that?" Mendy said, frowning up.

"I ain't saying we're boyfriend and girlfriend—but some people are saying it."

"You don't know what you're talking about. Why would anybody say that? We've been best friends since we were four and five years old. Why, my daddy pulled your teeth out for you. And your ma made my first Sunday communion dress. Your daddy helped build us a tree house. Ain't nobody that stupid to say we're boyfriend and girlfriend. We're like brother and sister. We're *blood* sister and brother, remember? At least we used to be."

Jeffrey hit his hand against the tree trunk. "Look, how old are you?" he asked.

"Don't be stupid. You know I'm twelve going on thirteen."

"And I'm fourteen. You know that means we're growing up."

"So?" Mendy said.

"So you don't get it, do you? Our parents think we do more than play when we're together—now."

"They're right," she said, scowling. "We do. We argue a lot more."

"Girl, wake up. They think we been kissing and stuff."

"Kissing?" She spit on the ground. "Ain't nobody in their right mind think we been kissing. Are you crazy? I ain't never even thought about kissing no boy. Why, if a boy tried to kiss me, I'd pop him upside the head. Yuck."

Jeffrey shook his head. He picked up a rock and threw it. A tree on the other side of the spring shook.

"You're serious, ain't you?" Mendy said, recognizing the worried look on his face. "*That's* what this is about? Well, I still don't see what that has to do with the Highlander School."

"Think about it, Mend. Folks are mad at Mr. Horton 'cause he lets whites and coloreds eat together and sleep in the same buildings. He up and hired a colored woman as the head teacher. Shoot, my ma heard he even lets coloreds swim with whites in the pond out there."

"That part is true," Mendy said, and immediately she regretted it. She remembered, too late, that Daddy had said not to tell anybody about the swimming at Highlander.

"You know good and well," Jeffrey continued, "it's illegal in Tennessee for whites and coloreds to do that kind of thing together. Ma says the law's going to start cracking down on white people who act like they love niggers."

Mendy's head shot up, her eyes glaring at Jeffrey. "What did you just say?"

"I ain't mean no harm. I was just telling you what Ma said, that's all."

Mendy stood up. Her stomach burned, like hot coals were steaming inside. No one had ever said that word to her face before. It made her furious. She wasn't even sure why. "Don't you ever say that word in front of me again," Mendy said through clenched teeth, her fists balled up. "You hear me?"

"Mend, I won't. But you live in a dream world. You don't know what it's like to have people picking on you 'cause you like the coloreds."

Mendy sat back down. All the air seemed to go out of her in a *whoosh*. She hadn't ever considered that people would pick on someone just for being friends with her. "I'm sorry. We don't have to be friends ever again," Mendy said. "You said so yourself."

"See, now you've gone and made me hurt you. Mend, please. Let's just deal with your problem right now. Actually, your problem *is* my problem—we're blood sister and brother, right?" He held out his hand for their secret handshake.

As Mendy took it, she looked at his hand next to hers. She'd never thought about him as a white boy before. Until now, he had always been just Jeffrey.

Jeffrey said, "Those men in the clearing, they're the KKK—the Ku Klux Klan."

"What do they do?" Mendy asked. Deep in the back of her mind, she remembered hearing her parents whispering something about the KKK.

"They don't like colored people. They threaten and hurt coloreds. They burn crosses in front of coloreds' houses to scare them if they get out of line." Jeffrey dropped his head. "They have hung coloreds, too. My daddy told me all about them. His daddy used to be one of 'em."

Mendy felt sick. This all sounded unbelievable to her. Why hadn't anyone ever told her any of this? "Jeffrey, have you seen this symbol of theirs—a circle with a cross inside it?" Mendy asked. "Do you know what it means?"

"That's the Cross Wheel. It's supposed to be the Christian cross in a circle of light. They also have the Blood Drop symbol that represents the blood of Jesus Christ. They say he was sacrificed for the white race." Jeffrey's voice was very small.

"Christian? Are you saying they're Christians?"

Jeffrey said, "They say they are."

"So why do they wear robes and pointed hats like that?" Mendy asked.

"It's so people won't know who they are, because the Klan's supposed to be a secret thing. And because, well, it ought to be that they are ashamed."

Mendy stared down at the dirt. She watched an ant crawl past her shoe. Finally she looked up at Jeffrey and said, "This sounds so scary to me."

"It *is* scary. This ain't nothing to play with," Jeffrey said.

"I'm worried about Mr. Horton, Jeffrey. And I'm

worried about Aunt Sis. Maybe those men will try to bother her again."

"I don't know, Mend. But if they did, it would be at night. They mostly 'ride' at nighttime."

"Then we need to talk to Aunt Sis. We better warn her while she's in her right mind."

They walked to Aunt Sis's without much talking. Twice they had to duck down off the road so nobody would see them together. Mendy tried to figure out why her daddy and mama hadn't told her all this themselves. But deep down, she knew. They were always trying to protect her from every hurt.

Aunt Sis was shading under the crabapple tree when they walked up. "Howdy, Mendy," she said, just like everything was normal. "Come sit a spell. Rest your feet. Who's that handsome young'un with you? Lord, that's the Whitehall boy, ain't it? You done growed up. I knows your whole family, boy. Come sit and talk to Aunt Sis," she said, patting a spot on the ground next to her.

Mendy said, "Aunt Sis, we have something serious to ask you about."

"Gw'on and ask hit," she said.

Mendy said, "Do you know anything about the KKK?"

"Sure I do. They meetin' in them woods over yonder. I know 'cause I heard noise and went to look. They seen me eyeing 'em. They come after me, too. Not 'fore I took one they stinking flags, though. Now I can't find it nohow, but I coulda *swore* I took it. I ain't even sure how I got home. I don' reckon they knew it was me, though, since they ain't come here yet." Aunt Sis paused and brushed a hand over her eyes. "Or maybe I only dreamed it. Maybe I ain't seen 'em a'tall, child."

Now Mendy understood what had happened. She said, "No, Aunt Sis. You saw 'em. I found you that night, hiding in a cave. I took the cloth from you and put you to bed."

"So 'tis true. Lord, child, I done almost thought I was off on one of my spells. Lordy, Lordy."

Jeffrey asked, "You know who any of those men were?"

"How I know? They's covering their cowardly faces. One of them's got a ring, though—big old silver ring with some triangle on it. I ain't forgetting that ring."

"I saw that ring!" Mendy said, remembering how it had glinted in the firelight. She'd almost forgotten that. She'd seen the ring and the man's shoes really good. "Aunt Sis," she said, "did you hear those men say anything about the Highlander School?"

"Yes'm. Scare me out of my wits, it did. They's gon' try something bye and bye."

Mendy's heart raced. "What do you mean, Aunt Sis?" Was the Klan planning something against Mr. Horton for real? Mendy felt fear grip her stomach. She and Jeffrey exchanged glances, and she could tell that Jeffrey was scared, too.

But when Mendy turned back to Aunt Sis, a faraway

look had come over her face. "Caleb, you hungry?" Aunt Sis asked Jeffrey. "That's you, ain't it, Caleb?"

Jeffrey looked puzzled.

"Don't worry," Mendy whispered to him. "She'll be all right. She's just a little confused right now." Mendy took Aunt Sis's hand. "Aunt Sis," she said, "Caleb's not here. This is Jeffrey."

"Lord, Caleb, you gon' run, ain't you? I see it in your face. Freedom coming soon."

"Let's go," Mendy said. "She'll be all right. She goes in and out like that, but she always comes back. Don't you, Aunt Sis?" Then Mendy looked into Aunt Sis's eyes. "And they won't bother you, Aunt Sis. I'm going to see to that." Mendy made up her mind. She would find out who those men were and make sure they got arrested before they hurt Aunt Sis or Mr. Horton.

Mendy and Jeffrey left Aunt Sis smiling under the apple tree.

CHAPTER 7
CIRCLE OF FIRE

"I'm going to do something to stop them," Mendy said as she and Jeffrey walked from Aunt Sis's toward the clearing.

"You mean *we're* going to do something, Mend."

"Good. You're in," Mendy said. "I think it's time we tell someone."

Jeffrey bit his lip. "I suppose we could tell my pa."

"But then he'll know we've been together. You might even get sent to that boys' school. I think we should tell the sheriff."

"Mend, what can we tell him? We don't really know what the Klan is planning, and we don't know who's involved. It's dangerous messing with the Klan. If we start accusing people without proof, our families could end up with crosses burning in the yard. Or worse."

"We'll just have to find out who the men are, then, and what they're up to."

"And how are we supposed to find that out, Mend? Ask them?"

"No. We need to spy on them next time they meet," Mendy said. "We can try to make out who they are. They might even take them hoods off. Maybe they'll talk about what they're planning on doing up at Highlander."

"I don't know, Mend. If they catch us spying, they might hurt us bad."

"*If* they catch us. But they ain't gonna see us. We know how to stay hidden in the woods."

"Have you forgot we ain't supposed to even be on Jeb Connor's land?" Jeffrey reminded Mendy. "If we do see something, we can't tell it."

"What's gotten into you? We don't have a choice. Daddy says if you see something wrong, it ain't right to do nothing."

"Yeah, but this is dangerous. We're just kids."

"Then stay here. Don't come with me," Mendy said, marching off into the woods.

Jeffrey raced after her.

When they reached the clearing, they were both out of breath. And the choking sulfur in the air made it even harder for them to breathe.

Mendy didn't need to check her trap—the skunk had sprayed. She didn't know when the skunk had sprayed, or why. But if it had sprayed while still in the trap, then whoever had picked up the bowie knife would be marked with skunk scent for days. If Mendy or Jeffrey met up with him anywhere, they'd know who he was for sure.

Before they left the clearing, Mendy and Jeffrey vowed to meet late that night at the edge of Jeb Connor's woods. They'd meet every night at the same time until the men returned to the clearing. They had to find out who the men were and tell the sheriff before Aunt Sis, Mr. Horton, or somebody else got hurt.

That evening Mendy leafed through her scrapbook, looking for courage. Her eyes landed on one of Mrs. Roosevelt's sayings that Mendy had never noticed before:

> *Discrimination does something intangible and harmful to the souls of both white and colored people.*

Mendy thought about the words. Then, just below them, she wrote words of her own:

> *Today I learned more about people in the world. Mama always said she wanted to protect me from every-thing, and I was never sure what she meant. But now I think she was talking about the meanness people do if you ain't the same color they are. It doesn't seem right. Maybe that's what Daddy learned about in the war.*

Maybe Daddy learned we should all be treated the same.
That's probably why he likes Mr. Myles Horton so much.
Mr. Horton treats Daddy like he's just as good as any
of the whites. Mr. Horton was the only white person
around here who hired Daddy to do his plumbing. But
now maybe I kind of understand Mama a little. She was
scared I might get hurt. Maybe Mama does love me.

Mendy sneaked out later that night and met up with
Jeffrey. They went to the woods, but the men did not come.
The next three nights were the same. Nothing.

On Friday, when the moonlight danced on the trees
and the mockingbird stopped singing, Mendy sneaked out
again. The house was completely quiet and Daddy wasn't
home yet. He'd called and said his job in Chattanooga was
taking longer than he'd expected.

As Mendy neared Mr. Connor's woods, she saw puffs
of smoke rising up out of the trees. The men were back.

Mendy met Jeffrey at the edge of the woods and they
hurried on together. They moved quietly through the
underbrush, staying off the path to keep themselves hidden.
The woods smelled pretty, fragranced with moonflower
and honeysuckle.

Nearer to the Taj, the smell of smoke filled their lungs.

Mendy and Jeffrey smeared mud on their hands and faces for camouflage and crept on. When the clearing came into view, Mendy almost stopped breathing out of fear. This was no game, like the cowboys and Indians she and Jeffrey used to play. This was real.

The crowd was bigger than before. There were at least fifteen white-robed men standing in a circle, maybe more. A few held up white flags with the red Cross Wheel. Tonight two men waved Confederate flags, and others held flaming torches high above their heads.

In the center of the clearing, Mendy could see a large wooden cross wrapped in white rags. Sticks were piled under it like a bonfire waiting to be lit. A man standing near it began yelling into a megaphone, "White is Right!" The other men pumped their fists into the air and shouted, "White is Right! White is Right! White is Right!"

Mendy couldn't see them clearly from her hiding place in the brush. She moved a few inches to the left, then a few more inches, closer and closer. She was almost at the edge of the path now, but at least some of the men were more visible.

One man yelled, "So what are we going to do about the commie witch?"

A lump as big as a bullfrog hopped into Mendy's throat. Who were they talking about? Mendy moved even closer to the path.

"I say a bunch of us ride out there and smash up the place."

Another man shouted, "No! We oughta burn a cross up at the Highlander to let them know we don't like it none. Give 'em a warning."

The man in the center said, "As the Exalted Cyclops of Dayton Klavern, I say we do nothing. Ain't no call to make ourselves exposed over no dang woman givin' a commie speech."

Mendy's eyes burned with tears. It couldn't be. They couldn't be talking about *her.*

"Well, I don't agree," another voice shouted. "I say we stop the speech, even if we have to blow the place up. Some of us is already planning, and we aim to do it. If any you boys wanna join us, just let me know. It's about time for fireworks 'round here."

A loud, foot-stomping cheer went up in the air. Dust devils, weirdly lit by the fire, caught in the air and whirled off into the bushes.

It took everything in Mendy's body not to gasp out loud. They were planning to bomb the Highlander Folk School while Mrs. Roosevelt was there!

When the cheering died down, the man with the megaphone ordered, "Circle formation. Dress right dress." The men stood up straight and made their circle even wider. Each man put his right hand out to touch the shoulder of the next person. It looked like a military drill.

Mendy watched, terrified by what she had heard. She had to keep the bombing from happening. Mendy tried to identify the man closest to her. Even through his white sheet, the silhouette seemed familiar somehow. She tried to get a look at his shoes, but she couldn't. Then she had a stroke of luck. The men began marching in a circle, chanting.

Slowly, each man passed into Mendy's view, only a few yards away. Though Mendy could see only the men's hands and shoes, she tried to find something unique that she could remember about each person. One man's nails had been bitten down to the nub. Another's hands were so filthy it looked like dirt was ground into his skin all the way past his wrists, and his brogans were like her daddy's but dustier, and one of the laces was knotted together where it had broken. Another man had long, thin fingernails like a woman's. Mendy recorded these details in her mind as the men marched round and round chanting "White Rule!" and pumping their fists into the air.

The blazing torches sent reflections dancing in the trees like the shadows of angels. Dust billowed up around the marchers' feet. The air hung heavy, like it could stop a body from breathing.

Mendy's position, almost out in the open, meant she could not move or even flinch without giving herself away, but her insides vibrated with fear. Mendy wanted to give Jeffrey a signal that she was all right but she dared not.

Her throat felt parched from the dust swirling in the air. She prayed she would not have to cough.

Suddenly the man with the megaphone barked, "About, face," and the men turned toward her. Then came the order, "Column. Right. March." The men formed a line and began to march toward the path.

Mendy fought back waves of nausea. *Oh God,* she thought. They were coming directly toward her, and there was nothing she could do.

The man at the head of the line, the man whose silhouette had seemed vaguely familiar, was on the path now, coming closer, closer. He looked down, and just for a second it seemed to Mendy that he stared right into her eyes. Mendy looked away. Her gaze rested on his shoes. She saw that he wore brown penny loafers, and he was so close that Mendy could see he had buffalo nickels wedged into them instead of pennies. Mendy could see every scuff and pick in the leather on the toes of his shoes.

Mendy was frozen with fear. In seconds he would step on her. Then, unbelievably, she saw him trip and topple to the side. Another man piled on top of him, then a third. The next man stopped to help them up. The man in the center yelled to them, "Halt. Fall back. Fall back in the circle. Let's have our new brothers say their pledge and get out of here."

The men moved back into the clearing. Mendy tried desperately to quiet her drumming heart and watch.

One robed man touched his torch to the wrapped cross. Mendy could see it was the man with the dusty brogans and grimy hands. As the sleeve of his robe fell away, she saw that the dark color went all the way up his arm.

Whoosh. The blaze engulfed the wooden cross. Cinders floated skyward, piercing the night like stars.

Each man put his right hand over his heart. The man with the megaphone shouted, "Brothers, repeat after me. 'By my own free will and instance I swear, by the mighty God, that I never to anyone will tell by a hint, sign, action, or word about the secrets, signs, handshakes, keywords, or ceremonies that belong to the Order, neither that I am a member of this Order, nor that I know a member. I will submit to the regulations for the Order and its commands.'"

After the men had repeated the pledge, they began shouting about defending and protecting the white race. Then Mendy heard one voice rise above the others, shouting, "I will kill any coon-dog–colored man, woman, or child to defend the white race."

Mendy closed her eyes and prayed. She couldn't bear to hear any more. She wanted to jump up and run away. She wanted this to be over. It felt like poisonous snakes were crawling in her stomach. For the first time in her life, she wished she were home in her bed, being a lady like Mama wanted her to be.

And now all her mama's fears made sense. Mama knew

that there were men who hated—men who hated enough
to kill anyone who wasn't white, even her daddy, her
mama, her brothers and sisters—even Mendy. She felt a
tear crawl down her muddy face.

When the last flicker of the men's torches had dis-
appeared through the forest, she heard Jeffrey whisper,
"You all right, Mend?"

Mendy couldn't find her voice. Jeffrey helped her
stand up. Her legs were stiff as boards. She was shaking
all over, and her teeth were chattering, as if she'd felt a
wind from the coldest place on earth. "Why do those
men hate colored people so?" she asked Jeffrey.

"I don't know, Mend," Jeffrey said. "But we got to
find out who they are and tell the sheriff. We've got
three days before Mrs. Roosevelt comes to Highlander.
We ought to be able to figure out some of them at least.
Tomorrow I'll meet you at McFee's General Store at
noon, 'round in the back. We can start there and see if
we can recognize anybody. Some of 'em is bound to live
in town or come to town on Saturdays."

Mendy headed home and quietly got into bed. The
room seemed lonelier than ever. She realized that she'd
never felt hatred before from anyone. Even when her
brothers and sisters were mad at her, it didn't feel like
those men had made her feel. Sometimes Mama and
Daddy had an argument, but Mendy could tell they still
loved each other. She had never known until tonight

that there were such people in the world. It was hard to believe that God let them be out there saying all those hateful things, and using his name too.

Mama was right—learning something new could hurt you. Those men hated her and her whole family. *Was* there something wrong with being a colored person?

Mendy tossed and turned for the few hours left of the night. She wished she could crawl in bed with Grandma or Clara. Finally she got out her scrapbook and reread Mrs. Roosevelt's saying about discrimination.

Mendy turned the page. She read another saying by Mrs. Roosevelt that she'd never paid much attention to before: *No one can make you feel inferior without your consent.* Mendy hugged the scrapbook until she fell asleep.

The next morning, when Mama called her, Mendy didn't want to get up. For some reason, knowing people hated her just because she was colored made her not want to move. *But you gotta move,* Mendy thought. Grandma had taught her that. *You always gotta move, even if your body don't feel up to going.* Mendy got up. She reread Mrs. Roosevelt's words. She decided she would not give those men consent. Being colored was just fine.

CHAPTER 8
REVELATIONS

After breakfast Mendy practiced the piano for an hour without being told. She discovered that the music soothed her. Then Mendy opened the Bible and read the Twenty-third Psalm: *The Lord is my Shepherd; I shall not want. He maketh me to lie down in green pastures* . . .

Daddy said whenever you needed a dose of bravery, you should read that and you'd be less afraid. Mendy needed courage now, because all she felt inside was fear. She was terrified to go into town and find out who in Cowan hated people just because of their color. What would she do when she faced those men? But she had to go meet Jeffrey. She couldn't let Mrs. Roosevelt down.

After breakfast Mendy asked Mama, "May I go play with Brenda Hatfield today?"

Mama turned around slowly, eyeing Mendy from her shoes to her neatly combed hair. "Say what?"

"I'd like to go play with Brenda," Mendy repeated. "You said I could."

Mama frowned. "Are you up to something, Mendy?"

"No, ma'am," Mendy said. "I'm bored, Mama, that's all."

"Well, all right. But don't stay too long. And don't go wandering off. You go straight there and come right back."

Mendy walked quickly toward town. She hated that she'd told Mama a fib. There was no way in the world she'd go play with Brenda Hatfield. That poor girl didn't know to play but one thing, a tea party. And Mrs. Hatfield kept her nose as high as a bird in the sky. Just because she and Reverend Hatfield were from Philadelphia, they thought the mountain folk were backward. But Mendy knew who was really backward, and it wasn't the mountain folk.

Stores lined both sides of Cowan's main street for two blocks. Mendy headed for the general store, careful to stay out of sight of anyone who knew Mama. Mendy slipped behind the store and hid. She and Jeffrey couldn't risk anybody seeing them together and telling their parents.

Finally Jeffrey showed up. He held out a small notepad and pencil. "Here, I bought you this. If we find anything out, we can write it down."

Mendy took the notepad. "Thanks, that's a good idea. Now you go that way, and I'll go this direction. We can both be on the lookout for anybody wearing that silver ring, or the shoes I told you about, especially the loafers."

"And we'll both keep our noses out for skunk," Jeffrey added. "Let's meet back here in an hour."

Mendy headed down the sidewalk, her eyes glued to the shoes of the people walking past her. She saw brogans, work boots, saddle shoes, high heels—but no men's loafers. She started to feel dizzy keeping her eyes on all those moving feet. How was she ever going to find what she was looking for this way? Then she had an idea.

Mendy walked up the street to the barbershop. The barbers were all white men, but three days a week they let a colored man shine shoes for tips outside on the sidewalk. If anybody could tell her who had the penny loafers, he could.

Uncle Steven was spitting on a brown shoe as Mendy walked up. She waited patiently until his customer left.

"Howdy, Miss Mendy," he said, smiling. "What you doing hanging 'round up here?"

"I got something important to ask you, Uncle Steven. Something secret. I've got to whisper it to you," Mendy said. He wasn't her uncle, but colored children called all the old people uncles and aunts.

"It must be top-secret if you got to whisper. Ask on't then."

Mendy cupped her hand over his ear and whispered.

He raised his eyebrows. "Why do you need to know that, young blood?"

Mendy was proud he called her that. It was a name

old men called young boys. Everybody colored knew that
Mendy could ride a horse, fish, or trap as good as any
boy around.

"I seen 'em, that's all, and I just want to know," she
said, hoping he wouldn't make her say more.

"Hmm. Let me see," he said, rubbing his mixed gray
beard. "Hit's two or three men in Cowan with them
penny loafers. There's three or four more in Hixson, and
a bushel of 'em up in Sewanee. But, now, you say he had
nickels wedged in his shoes instead of pennies. Right
now I can only reckon but one like that. That would be
Boyd D. Bryson. He's bad news to any colored man and
a good, close friend of that old Jeb Connor."

"Thank you, Uncle Steven," Mendy said.

Boyd D. Bryson sounded like the perfect match for
those shoes. And he was friends with Jeb Connor, who
owned the clearing. Mean old Mr. Connor must be in the
Klan, too. Until now Mendy had just thought he didn't
want coloreds on his land. Mendy stopped at the corner
and wrote *Boyd D. Bryson* and *Jeb Connor* on her notepad.

Next Mendy wanted to find the man with the grimy
hands and arms. Mendy tried to think what could make
somebody look like that. Sometimes Daddy's hands
looked all tar-greased black after he'd been blacksmithing,
but his hands didn't stay that way. It seemed like this man
was grimy all the way up to his elbows with some kind of
stain that didn't wash off.

Mendy leaned against the gray planks of a building and considered. What could those stains be? Grease, maybe. Brown, gunky grease. And hadn't his nails been all jagged? He must be a mechanic. That was it. She headed for the train yard. Maybe he fixed train engines. All the trains crossing the Cumberland to Chattanooga had to come through Cowan.

Mendy loved the trains. Even though she was in a hurry, when she got to the train yard she stopped a minute to watch the pushers, the engines that pushed trains over the steep grades of the Cumberland Mountains. Then, off to the side of the yard, Mendy spotted a man repairing an engine. His body was almost hidden under the engine, with just his legs sticking out from underneath.

Mendy moved quietly, like she did when she was in the woods, until she was close enough to see his shoes. He had on dusty brogans, just like the ones she'd seen in the clearing, but she couldn't tell if one of the strings was broken. Her heart pounded. She stepped back. Maybe she should hide behind something to watch him.

Suddenly he slid out from under the iron wheel. He sat up fast, so fast that Mendy didn't have a chance to run and hide.

"What you sneaking around here for, gal?" he asked. He unfolded himself and stood, rising higher and higher.

Mendy's eyes stretched wide. He was huge like an old oak in the woods, a tall mountain man with red hair and a bushy red beard. He was wiping his big hands on a greasy work cloth. Even without checking his hands or the strings in his shoes, Mendy knew he wasn't the man she was looking for. No one at the clearing had been this big.

"You hear me talking to you, gal?" the man said.

"Yes, sir. I was just looking for—looking for a man that Mr. Whitehall wanted to talk to," Mendy said, afraid to use her daddy's name in case this giant was in the KKK, too.

"What man?" he asked, looking down at her.

Mendy wondered if she looked like a small ant to him.

"I said, what man? You hard of hearing, gal?"

"No, sir. Uh, he just sent me down here to find a man that's got a brown stain on his hands and his nails all broken up," Mendy said, realizing how stupid that sounded.

Suddenly the man started laughing. "What in tarnation you talking about? He musta just been playing 'round wid you, gal. Ain't no man here like that. Now go on, git," the man said. He was still laughing as he walked away.

Mendy blew out a big sigh of relief. That was close.

But if the man she was looking for didn't work in the train yard, then where? Maybe something farmers grew had stained his hands. She ticked off crops that grew in the area—cotton, corn, oats—but none of those things would stain a man's hands. What could it be?

Suddenly, like the moon rising full on a dark night, the answer came to her. There was only one person who did a job that would make his hands look like that. She headed for the stables.

In the back of the stables, where people got their workhorses shod and their wagons fixed and such, old man Benefield tanned hides. He made leather from all kinds of hides, even from snakeskin, and he used dyes to color the leather—dyes that wouldn't wash out.

Mendy didn't want him to see her, so she went around to the back of the building. She knew, since it was simmering hot out, that the back door would be flung wide open. She was in luck. Through the back doorway, she saw Mr. Benefield dipping hides in a large barrel.

Mendy peeped around the door, but she was too far away to see his hands or his shoes. She looked around to see if anyone was watching her. No one was in sight. Sliding her body against the building, she moved under the window. She checked one more time to see if anyone was watching her and then peered in. *Bingo.*

Mr. Benefield wore dusty brogans with one string mended. And each time he lifted the leather up out of the barrel, Mendy could see the brown dye dripping off his hands. His arms were dark all the way to his elbows.

Suddenly, Mendy felt like she was choking; right then and there it felt like someone had put his hands around her neck. She had known Mr. Benefield all her life. Grandma had birthed his oldest boy before Mendy was even born, because white Dr. Pritchard had been away.

Every Thanksgiving Mr. Benefield donated a turkey to
the colored church for the needy.

Mendy squeezed her eyes shut. Maybe she had made
a mistake. She tried to recall the scene in the clearing.
Was the broken string on the left brogan? Was the man
under that robe Mr. Benefield's size? She pictured the
man stretching out his stained arms to light the cross.
She looked at Mr. Benefield again. It was him, all right.

Mendy backed away from the window. She turned an
old tin bucket over and sat down on it. Her eyes filled
with tears. She pulled out her pencil and wrote name
number three, *Mr. Benefield*. A tear dropped down onto
her pad. She wiped her eyes with the back of her hand.

She took a deep breath and straightened her shoulders. There was no time for crying. She had to keep going.
She decided she would look for whoever had been sprayed
by the skunk. But how to find him? Maybe she could ask
some of the washerwomen. No, they'd probably go tell
Mama. Mendy decided to just walk along the street and
try to catch a whiff of skunk. Even if the man had thrown
away the clothes that got sprayed, the skunk smell would
linger on him.

Mendy started in front of the post office. There was
a good cluster of people there, and anyway, she had always
liked passing it because the United States flag fluttered in
the wind. Mendy loved the flag because Daddy told her
he had fought in the war to protect it. She passed people

who smelled of tobacco, cement dust, lilac, spices, and plain rancid body odor. This wasn't such a pleasant plan, she decided.

Just then, Mendy caught sight of a clock through a storefront and saw that her time was up. She rushed off to meet Jeffrey, feeling pretty good that she had three names. Maybe Jeffrey had found more.

Surely they could go to the sheriff now, she thought. Three or four names ought to give him enough evidence to start investigating. The men might deny everything, but if the sheriff questioned them all, maybe they'd tell different stories and the sheriff would catch them in a lie.

Mendy ran back toward the general store. As she passed Cowan's only shoe store, she saw Mr. Franks coming out. He was a big man who smiled a lot and sometimes gave children horehound candy. Mendy waved to him and ran toward his wagon. He was climbing up on the seat when Mendy got a whiff of him. She slowed to a snail's pace.

"Hey, gal. Come on over here. I got some candy for you," he called to her. Mendy didn't move. The sight and smell of him now made her feel sick on the stomach. She quickly turned and walked the other way. She heard him hit his mules and say, "Gid up." She listened as the hoofbeats moved away. Mendy could feel her heart breaking open.

She had always thought Mr. Franks liked the coloreds,

but now she knew the truth. She sat down on the wooden steps of a storefront and added *Mr. Leo Franks* to her list. He had skunk smell all over him.

Mendy got up. There was no time for feeling sad. She had four names now! She was so eager to tell Jeffrey that she started running. By the time she reached the corner near the general store, she was racing so fast that she didn't even see Jeffrey. She ran smack into him and almost knocked him down.

He stumbled back, and Mendy reached out to keep him from falling. For a split second they were actually holding hands. Embarrassed, Mendy let his hand go as soon as he balanced himself. They both looked around quickly, then ducked behind the store.

"Sorry," Mendy said. "I was running because I got a name to go with the loafers—Boyd D. Bryson. And he's friends with guess who—Jeb Connor." Then she told him about Mr. Benefield and Mr. Franks. "What did you get?"

"You did good. I got two names," Jeffrey said. "One was a man with the tattoo of an eagle on his arm. That one was easy. He's a mountain man from Dayton. And the other one is somebody that's gonna surprise you."

"Who? Who is it?" Mendy's heart pounded. She didn't want any more surprises like Mr. Benefield and Mr. Franks.

"You know the man with the long fingernails like a woman's? Well, I got a good look, and I know who it is, all right."

Mendy moved closer, "Who is it, Jeffrey? You look like you seen a ghost or something."

"I didn't want to believe it myself, Mend. It's Mr. Archie Poole, the principal of the white high school."

Mendy gasped, "You mean the *principal* hates colored people? But isn't he your pa's friend?"

"So what?" Jeffrey said. "Pa don't know he's with the Klan. Only we know it."

Mendy could see that Jeffrey looked as sad as she felt. She said, "Let's go to the sheriff. This ought to be enough names to get him started arresting people. He'll make sure nothing happens to Mr. Horton and Mrs. Roosevelt."

"Hold on, Mend," Jeffrey said. "Maybe we should think about what we're doing. Mr. Poole, Mr. Connor—those are two of the biggest names in town."

"There ain't no time to think," Mendy argued. "Mrs. Roosevelt's coming in two more days. We need to tell the sheriff *now*."

Jeffrey finally nodded. "But we can't go to the sheriff together," he said. "My pa will kill me if he finds out I'm with you. And besides that, it'd look mighty suspicious to folks if you and me went marching into the sheriff's office together."

"Yeah, you're right," Mendy admitted. "But I want to be there to back you up. I know what. I noticed a big pile of crates stacked up behind the jail, right by the sheriff's back window. I'll climb up there and wait. You go into the sheriff's office and try to get him alone. Then bring him over to the window. That way we can both talk to him and nobody'll see us together."

Jeffrey nodded. "It sounds crazy, Mend, but it just might work."

"What'll we say if the sheriff asks how we ended up on Jeb Connor's land?"

Jeffrey thought a moment. "We can say that we was fishing out by the stream one evening, the part that runs on Miss Sis's land. And your mare took off into the woods. While we was looking for her, we stumbled onto the men before they put on their robes and hoods."

"You think he'll believe us?"

"Let's hope so."

They split up, and Mendy sneaked around to the back of the jail. She climbed carefully up the shaky pile of crates and crouched on top, keeping her head just below the window. She could hear the sheriff moving around in his office. Then she heard the door open and shut. Surprised that Jeffrey had gotten there so fast, she peeped up into the window. Her breath caught in her throat.

It wasn't Jeffrey who had just walked into the office, it was the deputy sheriff. Mendy didn't know him that well—she didn't even know his name—but she'd seen those shoes before.

CHAPTER 9
MORE BAD NEWS

The deputy talked louder than the sheriff did, but they both were keeping their voices low. Mendy strained to make out what they were saying. Her heart sounded like a drum in a parade.

"What you gon' do about it?" she heard the deputy asking. His voice sounded tense.

"Why, buddy, I just decided to take my vacation next week. That way, when the boys hit the place with their fireworks on Tuesday, well, I'll be on my holiday."

Mendy could hear them laughing. She couldn't believe it. The sheriff already knew about the bombing, and he wasn't going to stop it. Mendy felt cold all over. The sheriff *couldn't* let something like that happen, not to the wife of the former President of the United States. Could he?

Then she heard the deputy say, "You know what? You doing the right thing. Let me read this to you. Come right out of the *Chattanooga News-Free Press:*

"The Highlander Folk School has earned its bad reputation over the years as a result of its left-wing programs, the Communist taint of its leadership, and the disgraceful conduct of school leaders." Mendy could hear the newspaper crackle as the deputy turned the page. *"More recently, attention has been centered on the folk school because of its emphasis on forcing racial integration and the accompanying*—uh—*deteration*—"

"Deterioration," the sheriff interrupted.

"I got it," the deputy said, sounding annoyed. Then he continued reading: "—*of harmony and disruption of goodwill upon the South. It is a gathering place for leaders in agitation of racial issues.* Dah, dah, dah. *Mrs. Roosevelt's name long has been linked with the school, she having been one of its early contributors and sponsors.* Got any doubts now that we're doing right? We gotta let folks stand up and fight for their country."

Mendy couldn't even swallow. She heard the door opening and peeked in again. It was Jeffrey. Mendy had to warn him. She stood higher on the crates and flung her hands in front of the window. Jeffrey didn't even look. As a last resort, she whistled one of the bird signals they knew, and he glanced up toward her. But so did the others. Mendy ducked out of sight.

At that moment, the crates gave way. The splitting of the wooden slats echoed in her ears as she crashed to the ground.

Mendy could hear the deputy shouting, "What's that

little Negra girl doing up in the window spying?" Mendy heard them racing out the front door as she scrambled to get up. Thank goodness the jail had no back door.

Mendy jumped up and took off running as fast as she could. She hoped that Jeffrey had understood her warning. She frantically whispered the Twenty-third Psalm as she ran down Main Street and out of town.

Mendy didn't stop running until she got home. Once she was in the yard, relief washed over her—but only for a second. Reverend Hatfield's car was parked in the yard.

Could anything else go wrong? Mendy wondered as she stared at the Hatfield's fancy blue Buick. She thought about hiding out at Aunt Sis's until things blew over. But what if the sheriff figured out who she was and came looking for her? He'd give Mama a real bad time if she couldn't tell him where Mendy was. No, she'd have to face the music, like Daddy always said. Mendy squared her shoulders and marched toward the house. A soldier stands up for what he believes in. How many times had Daddy told her that?

Mendy didn't know why the Reverend Hatfield had shown up. But one thing was for sure: Mama would have asked him about Mendy. And once Mama found out that Mendy hadn't gone to play with Brenda, she would be furious. Mendy took a deep breath, preparing to face Mama. But when she stepped through the door, her mouth fell open. Mama was sitting on the sofa, and she was crying. Mendy had never seen Mama cry before, and it made her hurt so bad inside she wanted to go get her own switch for the whipping. She had embarrassed Mama again.

"Mama," Mendy said, coming into the room, "I'm sorry. I didn't mean to—"

"Sit down, Mendy," her mama said. "I have something to tell you."

Mendy sat down close to Mama on the couch. Mama was twisting a handkerchief in her hands. Suddenly the house seemed too still. "Where's Li'l Ben?" Mendy asked, sensing now that something was seriously wrong.

"My wife took him home," Reverend Hatfield answered in his Philadelphia accent. "How did your clothes get all messed up, young lady?"

Mama looked at the reverend. "She's a mountain girl. She gets like that. It's all right for her to get dirty sometimes."

Mendy was speechless. Had Mama just defended her being a tomboy? Yes, something was wrong, something bigger than her not going to play with Brenda.

"Why you crying, Mama?" Mendy asked, wishing she didn't have to know.

"Mendy, your daddy got sick in Chattanooga."

"What?" Mendy said, too loudly. "Daddy is never sick."

"People get sick," Reverend Hatfield said. "Your daddy
has a bad fever. Nobody knows for sure what it is. They
had to take him to the hospital."

"I want to see Daddy, Mama," Mendy said. Tears
slipped down her face. "I want to be with Daddy."

"You can't go, Mendy. Reverend Hatfield is going to
drive me to Chattanooga. You're going to have to stay at
the Hatfields'. I need you to take care of Li'l Ben for me."

"I wish Grandma was here. She would heal Daddy—
right, Mama? Isn't that right? Grandma could heal anybody," Mendy shouted.

Reverend Hatfield said, "Nobody can heal but God.
It's in God's hands now."

Mendy said, "God lets people have healing in their
hands, too. Grandma taught me that. Didn't she, Mama?"

"Your grandma was a heathen, young lady. Only
superstitious, uneducated people believe such things,"
Reverend Hatfield said, shaking his head.

"Reverend!" Mama exclaimed. "Please, that's her
grandma you're talking about."

"Sister Thompson, I'm disappointed in you. You should
be ashamed, allowing your daughter to hear that mumbo-
jumbo nonsense. It's sinning. The Devil will—"

"Reverend, that's enough. You're in my house," Mama
said. "Nobody calls my husband's mother a heathen. Not
even you. Please leave. I'll come by your place and pick up
my son. And then I'll make do. Only a heathen would say

such a thing to a child about her own grandma."

"But, Sister—"

"I'd just like you to go." Mendy's mama stood up and opened the screen door. "I'll be by soon to pick up Li'l Ben. We might be nothing but simple mountain folk, but at least we have common sense and manners. Thank you for coming by, Reverend."

The reverend walked stiffly through the door. Mendy got up and hugged her mama. She couldn't ever remember feeling so proud of Mama. "Everything will be all right, Mama. You'll see. Li'l Ben and I can stay over at Aunt Sis's house."

Mama sat down on Grandma's rocker and cried into her hands.

Mendy went to the bathroom and got a wet towel. "Here, Mama," she said, wiping her mother's face gently. "I love you, Mama. And you know what? I'm going to grow up to be a fine lady just like you want me to be."

Her mama looked up and smiled. "Thank you, Mendy," she said. "You're already a fine young lady." She hugged Mendy, and they both cried into each other's shoulders.

Mendy helped her mama pack. They put Mama's things into the only suitcase, since she was going on the train. Then Mendy got her things together along with Li'l Ben's and put them in a large paper bag.

"Mendy," Mama said when they were all packed, "I think maybe you should stay with one of the other church members. Aunt Sis's house is barely big enough for her. And you know she gets touched in her mind sometimes."

"Mama, I love Aunt Sis and she loves me. Besides, this way I'll be close by to take care of Tandy and the chickens and the dogs. We'll be fine. Li'l Ben and I can sleep on the floor on a pallet and pretend we're camping out. Li'l Ben loves to do that. Remember?"

"Sure, honey. I remember."

Mendy felt almost happy. Mama had called her "honey." She usually only called Daddy and Clara "honey." Mendy helped Mama pack a picnic lunch for the train, and they went to pick up Li'l Ben.

Reverend Hatfield was all huffy like a blowfish when they got there, but Mendy didn't care. And Mama, she didn't seem to care either.

⁓

By the time evening shadows were falling, Mama was on the train to Chattanooga, and Mendy and Li'l Ben were riding Tandy toward Aunt Sis's. As they rode along, Mendy said a prayer for Daddy. Then she let herself think about the earlier events of the afternoon.

What had happened after she left the jail? Would the sheriff come looking for her? More important, what could she and Jeffrey do now to stop the Klan's plans? There were only two days left before Mrs. Roosevelt's speech.

Mendy had no one to turn to. There was only one hope left, she realized, and that was for Jeffrey to tell his pa about the Klan. Maybe Jeffrey could manage to leave Mendy out of the story. Either way, though, his pa would believe Jeffrey, Mendy was sure.

Her worry eased a little. She knew Jeffrey. He would tell his pa. And Mr. Whitehall would do the right thing. Daddy always said Mr. Whitehall was a good man.

When Mendy and Li'l Ben reached the cabin, Aunt Sis was happy to see them and in her right mind. She gave them supper, and they all went to bed right after. Mendy hadn't even realized how exhausted she was until she lay down on the pallet beside Li'l Ben. He hugged Mendy around the neck and fell off to sleep even before she did. It felt good to take care of him.

Mendy fell asleep praying that her daddy was fine. She hoped that Jeffrey was all right, too, and that he had talked to his pa. Mr. Whitehall would see to it that the Klan didn't bother Mrs. Roosevelt. Mendy was sure of that.

CHAPTER 10

ALL ALONE

The next morning, Mendy set the table while Aunt Sis cooked grits. All through breakfast, Mendy kept glancing out the window to make sure the sheriff wasn't coming.

Once the dishes were washed up and the kitchen floor swept, Aunt Sis handed Ben a tiny corncob pipe. "Here, Li'l Ben," she said. "'Member how I showed you to blow bubbles out of here? Here's some soap water. Go outside and play with it while I speak on your sister."

Aunt Sis waited until Ben got settled out on the porch. Then she turned to Mendy. "Now," she said, "what come of you and that boy?"

"What do you mean?" Mendy asked. She held her breath, hoping that word hadn't gotten around about her being at the jail yesterday.

"I mean they's saying you and that boy was holding hands in broad daylight. I ain't got to tell you, some folks is riled up. Even the white folk that don't usually mess with the coloreds is saying that's the very thing they scared of. You young'uns know better'n be seen doing something like that, especially after what's been going on in the woods yonder. You want to see your folks swinging from a tree?"

Mendy's heart felt like a rock skipping across a stream. "We did no such thing," she shouted. "They are lying about me. And him."

"Lying ain't no proper word to speak to your elder, young'un. I done heard the sheriff even saw you trying to get a peek at the boy through the jailhouse window."

"Ma'am?" Mendy said. "The sheriff said that? You sure?"

"'Course I'm sure. Old Pete that drives the rolling store told me late yestiddy. Story is, that boy told the sheriff you was sweet on him and you wouldn't quit following him around. He was coming to the sheriff to make you stop. But his pa said he'd take care of it."

So that's what Jeffrey had said to the sheriff. Well, good. That meant Jeffrey didn't tell him what they knew about the Klan. And if Jeffrey's pa said he'd take care of it, maybe that was a signal to let Mendy know that everything would be all right. Mr. Whitehall would find a way to stop the bombing, to warn Mr. Horton and Mrs. Roosevelt. Maybe he would talk to the sheriff in Monteagle.

Mendy felt at peace for the first time since she found

the cigar. She'd been right: Jeffrey and his pa were taking care of the Klan and everything would be fine. Now she could concentrate on praying that Daddy would get well.

The next morning, though, Mendy woke up with a strange feeling inside. Something was wrong. She decided it wouldn't hurt to find Jeffrey and make sure everything *was* taken care of. "Aunt Sis, I've got to go off for a little while and take care of the animals at home. Do you mind keeping an eye on Li'l Ben?" she asked.

"No, child. Me and Li'l Ben gwan' be just fine." Aunt Sis took Li'l Ben by the hand. "Come on, baby, I'll give you some more soap water, and me and you can blow some bubbles in the corncob pipe. How 'bout that?"

Mendy mounted Tandy and headed toward home. When she got there, she tied Tandy up and quickly tended to the dogs and the chickens. Then she walked straight to Jeffrey's house. His pa's truck wasn't there, but Jeffrey's bike was around back. That's where he kept it if he wasn't planning on going anywhere. Mendy left a note in their secret code under the rock near the clothesline. She asked Jeffrey to meet her at the hog trough on the far edge of his pa's land. His pa rarely came out there except at hog-killing time. It was one of their safest meeting places.

Mendy threw some pebbles at Jeffrey's bedroom

window, hoping he was still in bed. Then she turned and ran as fast as she could. She didn't want his ma to see her sneaking around.

Mendy sat under a tree downwind of the hogs and waited for Jeffrey. Finally she saw him walking up the hill. He was walking real slow, his head hung down, his arms behind his back.

"Jeffrey, over here," she called to him. "What's the matter?"

"I've got some bad news, Mend," he said when he reached her. "Really bad."

"Don't worry, I know what you told the sheriff about me and I don't mind. That was quick thinking. I'm just glad you didn't tell them about the Klan. And I already figured out what your pa meant when he said he'd take care of it himself."

"Mend, stop it. I don't know what you're talking about." Jeffrey wouldn't look at her.

Mendy felt as if she couldn't breathe. "You *didn't* tell your pa about the Klan?"

"I told my pa," Jeffrey said. His head dropped lower. He still held his arms behind him.

"Well, that's great. I figured you did. My daddy says your pa ain't like the rest of them. Daddy always talks about how your pa was the only one who thanked him when he came back from the war—"

"Mend, shut up a minute and listen. This is the worst

thing that's ever happened in my whole life."

Mendy sat still and waited for him to go on. Was his pa going to send him away for real?

"I talked to the sheriff about the Klan's raid on the Highlander."

"Oh, no! They're in on it, Jeffrey. Why do you think I was giving you signals through the window?" Mendy stopped finally and paid attention to the look on Jeffrey's face. "Wait a minute, they ain't making trouble for your pa, are they?"

"No, Mend. In fact, the sheriff and his deputy told *me* about the raid. They thought I'd be happy about it."

"Why would they think that?" Mendy said, frowning.

"Well, you know, I told them you was following me around. They thought I wanted them to get you off my back, and they said they'd be happy to oblige. They said your daddy's been uppity ever since he came back from the war. They told me your daddy's been going to them meetings up at the Highlander and hanging out with the whites like he was just as good as them. They said they was going to get your daddy one day, too."

Mendy felt sick. "I'm *glad* my daddy ain't here, then," she whispered. "Because if he was here, I might have told him about the raid. And then maybe he would have done something about it and gotten hurt. But, Jeffrey, I still don't understand why the sheriff would tell *you* the Klan's secret plans? Do you?"

"It's simple, Mend," Jeffrey said. He kicked at the dirt. "All I can say is, I got to leave this alone. I can't help you no more."

Mendy jumped up, glaring into his face. "Why on earth not? You kidding, right? You *know* how important this is."

"Mend, don't make me tell you why. Please."

"No. You're going to tell me. You scared what they'll do to you? To me? Tell me," she said, shoving her finger into his chest.

Jeffrey didn't push her away. He just stood, head hanging low, hands clasped behind him. "All right, all right," he said finally. He sighed deeply and looked into her face. "It's my pa. Mend, my pa is in on it, too."

"Your pa ain't in on this, Jeffrey," Mendy said, taking a step back, her face burning hot. "That's just what the sheriff wants you to think. That's all."

"No, Mend, it ain't that."

"Okay, so what exactly did your pa say when you told him?"

"He said for me to stay out of it. That it ain't my business. And he forbid me to go near Myles Horton's place tomorrow."

"That don't mean he's in on it. Maybe he's just trying to protect you. My daddy would tell me the same thing." Mendy stared at Jeffrey, water pushing up in her eyes. He was scaring her now.

"No, Mend," Jeffrey continued, looking back down at the ground.

Suddenly the hogs squealed and grunted behind them. Mendy turned to see what the ruckus was about, but it was just two hogs squabbling. When she turned back, he said, "Recognize these?"

He had brought his hands out from behind him and was holding two shoes up to her. They were the shoes, the penny loafers Mendy had seen in the clearing. They had the same nickels, the same scratches on the right side, the same picks on the toes of the shoes. There was no doubt.

"Where did you get those shoes?" Mendy said, lowering her voice as if someone might hear her.

Jeffrey said, under his breath, "I guess Mr. Steven didn't tell you *everyone* in Cowan who has penny loafers."

Looking down at the shoes now, Mendy remembered the man staring at her in the clearing, as though he could look into her eyes. His eyes—they were glassy blue. Jeffrey's pa's eyes were the same color. Mendy wanted to die. She said, "I'm so sorry, Jeffrey."

"I'm sorry, too. I've got to go," he said, clutching the shoes to his chest.

"Wait!" Mendy said. "Nothing's changed. We still have to stop the raid. This ain't something we can just forget about. Even if it is your pa, we at least have to warn the Highlander people."

"I can't go against my own pa, Mendy Anna Thompson. Not even for you."

"Jeffrey, please. Even if it means people get killed?"

"Your daddy killed people in the war. Was that right? I just can't go against my pa. Now leave me alone. I feel bad enough."

Mendy wanted to scream at him, but she didn't. She watched him walk back down the hill. She glanced over at the hogs. Human beings weren't much better than hogs, she thought as she watched them clambering over each other to get to the slop. "Sometimes I don't think God made humans," she said to the hogs. "Sometimes I just can't believe it."

CHAPTER 11

THE ROAD TO MONTEAGLE

Mendy stomped all the way home. What could she do? All the sheriffs in Tennessee were probably just like the Cowan sheriff, she thought. The world needed to do better than the whites sticking with the whites and the coloreds sticking with the coloreds. Mendy wiped her tears away. She hadn't even realized she was crying.

Then it struck her that not *all* the whites were sticking with whites. Wasn't that why the Klan hated Mr. Myles Horton and Mrs. Roosevelt—because they was trying to get the whites and the coloreds to be friends?

Mendy walked home on automatic. Her head pounded like a hammer was banging inside her skull. As Mendy's house came into view, she thought of one more thing she could do to warn Mr. Horton. Mendy climbed through her bedroom window—she didn't have a key to the front door—and walked through the silent house to the kitchen.

The telephone sat on the counter. She got out the thin telephone book and looked up the Highlander Folk School. She really hadn't ever made a call. Not that many people she knew had telephones; Daddy just used the telephone for business. She dialed the number for the Highlander School, her hand shaking.

A woman with a pleasant voice answered, "Hello. Highlander Folk School."

"May I speak to Mr. Myles Horton?" Mendy asked.

"He's out of town. May I help you?"

Mendy hesitated, thinking of Mr. Benefield, Mr. Franks, and Mr. Whitehall. She didn't know what to say. The woman on the phone could be a part of the Klan for all she knew. Mendy couldn't trust any white person except Mr. Horton. And he wasn't there.

She wasn't even sure what she'd say to Mr. Horton. Would he believe her? She didn't really have any proof— just a few names, and two of them were the most respected men in Cowan. And, much as she hated to think it, another was Jeffrey's pa. Mendy said, "No, thank you," and hung up the phone.

Mendy racked her brain for anyone else to call. What about Miss May Justus? Daddy said she was a fine white woman. She was often at Highlander when Mendy went there to swim. Miss Justus wrote children's books, and once she had told Mendy that one day she was going to write a children's book that had the wonderful colored children in it. Mendy remembered how proud that had made her feel. She needed that feeling now.

Mendy looked up Miss Justus's name in the phone book. There was no listing. Mendy's heart sank. What else could she do? She walked into her bedroom and spotted her scrapbook lying wide open on the bed. Had Mama been looking at it? Mendy picked up the scrapbook and read the saying by Mrs. Roosevelt on the open page: *A woman is like a tea bag. You never know how strong it is until it's in hot water.*

Well, Mendy was in hot water now. Trouble with a capital *T* had come to her, and she didn't know what to do. She sat on the bed and tried to think of something. Her glance landed on Grandma's picture on the dresser top. Suddenly Mendy knew what Grandma would do if she were here. Mendy decided it was the only choice left. She just hoped she wasn't too late.

Mendy hastily grabbed a long-sleeved shirt and went out to the barn. She hitched Tandy to the dray, a low, heavy haul wagon. She loaded six steel traps into the dray—three small Victor traps used to catch rabbits and squirrels and three larger ones meant for foxes and coons. She added a pickax, a shovel, a flashlight, gloves for handling the traps, and lots of rope. She paused a moment, considering what else she needed. She loaded her own rusty red wagon onto the dray, too. She got two of her daddy's hunting knives from his hunting box and stuck them in her belt.

Now she was ready. She just needed to check on Aunt
Sis and Li'l Ben, and then she'd be on her way.

By the time she got to Aunt Sis's cabin, the sunset had
spread out in oranges and purples, wide like the hands of
God. Mendy looked up at the sky and wished the whole
world could feel the way she did when she saw the sky
this beautiful. God made the sky to be seen equally by
all people. Mendy took the sunset as a sign that she was
doing the right thing.

Mendy went into the cabin and found Aunt Sis rocking
Li'l Ben to sleep. Mendy was thankful that Aunt Sis was
in her right mind and seemed to be doing better lately. If
Mendy didn't make it back, Aunt Sis would take care of
Li'l Ben until Mama and Daddy got home.

Aunt Sis had left Mendy some chicken and dumplings
on the woodstove. Mendy didn't feel hungry, but she ate
to keep Aunt Sis from getting suspicious. While she sat at
the table, Mendy took her notepad from her pocket and
wrote a short letter.

Dear Mama and Daddy,

*Daddy, I hope you're feeling better when you
read this. I have prayed you would get well. I know
you wouldn't like what I'm going off to do. You would
say it's too dangerous, and Mama, you would say it
wasn't ladylike. But I think Grandma would be
proud if she was here. Aunt Sis is doing fine so I'm*

*not worried about Li'l Ben or I'd take him someplace
else. Aunt Sis loves him, and I know she wouldn't
hurt him, even in her wrong mind. Remember I love
you both.*

   *I am going to the Highlander School to make sure
that Mrs. Anna Eleanor Roosevelt is safe. Wish me luck.*
                                    Your daughter,
                                    Mendy, Wild Trapper

Mendy read the note to herself. She looked out into
the darkness. The moon was bright enough to light up the
tops of the trees. Another good omen. She would leave
the note for Aunt Sis to give to Mama and Daddy when
they came home. Aunt Sis couldn't read, so Mendy's plan
would remain a secret until Mama and Daddy saw the
note. If Mendy weren't back by then, they would know
something had gone wrong with her plan.

   Aunt Sis put Li'l Ben down in her own bed instead
of on the pallet. She said, "Mendy, sometimes we just got
to do what's right. I'm going on to bed now."

   Mendy's head shot up from the note. Did Aunt Sis know
that she was planning to sneak out? No, she couldn't know.
Mendy lay down on the pallet and pretended to sleep.

   Soon she heard Aunt Sis snoring lightly. Mendy got up
quietly and slipped outside. She untied Tandy and hitched
her to the dray. Mendy was shaking. It felt like barbed
wire was balled up inside her stomach.

Monteagle was a long ways away, up the mountain. Danger lurks in the mountains at night. And now Mendy could agree with Mama, going to Grundy County meant trouble with a capital *T* for sure. No coloreds had ever lived in that county. The saying was, if you was colored, don't let the sun go down on you in Grundy County. Mendy was afraid, but that wouldn't stop her. Daddy always said fear could not stop a person from doing what they had a call to do.

Mendy set off down the winding dirt road. She held the reins tightly as the dray rumbled along. A coon crossed Mendy's path, his eyes glaring up at her like lit marbles in the dark. Mendy slapped the reins so that Tandy would move on faster.

Mendy shuddered as she listened to the familiar sounds of nighttime in the Cumberland Gap. She tried to focus her mind on the beautiful lightning bugs dotting the landscape of hardwood forests and tobacco and cotton fields.

Soon she passed the fork in the road near where Grandma had tended a bed of wild ginseng, down below in a crevice. Grandma used to take Mendy to the crevice some nights, with just a lantern and a shotgun. Grandma believed that a moonlit night was the best time to rack the herbs she tended deep in the woods. Grandma had showed Mendy how to tend ginseng. She had given Mendy ginseng to taste, and many other healing plants, too—

quinine root, catnip, horehound, and sassafras. Grandma said the best way to know the healing qualities of a root or herb was to use it yourself. Leastways, Mendy thought now, if she got hurt tonight she'd know how to tend herself.

In a low whisper, Mendy started singing Daddy's song about the heavenly nights, but she couldn't remember all the words. She needed to be brave, she told herself. She recited the Twenty-third Psalm over and over, until she finally came to the single rusty chain stretched across the entrance to the Highlander property. It wasn't much to keep people out. Beside it stood a sign that read *ALL ARE WELCOME AT HIGHLANDER*.

Mendy didn't want to take the noisy dray on the road leading up to the school. She pulled the mare and dray off into the woods, down by a little brook. Mendy climbed down, unhitched Tandy, and tied her to a tree close to the brook so she could drink if she was thirsty. Then Mendy pulled her small red wagon from the dray and piled her traps and tools into it. Finally she put on her long-sleeved shirt. It made her sweat, but it would protect her from chiggers and ticks. "Tandy, you must be quiet," Mendy whispered to her. "I'll be back for you."

Mendy had no idea how long it would take her to do what she'd come to do. But she would not leave until she'd done it. Mendy Anna Thompson never abandoned her friends. And Mrs. Roosevelt was a friend, not only to her, but to all colored people.

For a moment, Mendy wished that Jeffrey were here with her. But then she recalled another of Mrs. Roosevelt's sayings: *A woman will always have to do better than a man in any job she undertakes.*

Mendy decided she was prepared to do just that.

CHAPTER 12

WILD TRAPPER

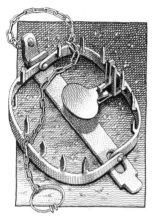

At night, the forest looks different than it does in the daylight. Mendy shined her flashlight into the dark tangle of trees and bushes until she found the trail, so faint that it was little more than a deer path. She hoped the sound of her rusty wagon would not carry too far. At least this part of the Highlander woods was pretty well isolated.

Mendy drew a mental map of the property. Last summer, while Daddy fixed the school's plumbing, Mendy had roamed the Highlander woods. She knew them well.

Right now, she was at the top of a rocky bluff hundreds of feet above the pond where she used to swim. Far below, on the other side of the pond, was the little cluster of buildings that made up the Highlander Folk School. Mendy knew that if anyone wanted to sneak up on those buildings, there was only one way to do it. A person would have to come through these woods, just the way she was doing now, and then pick his way down the left side of the bluff. Any other approach to the buildings was wide open and offered no cover.

Near the trail's entrance, Mendy checked the ground and the tree branches. She found no sign that anyone had passed this way recently, so she knew the Klansmen hadn't been here yet. But Mendy was confident that they'd be coming this way before morning to set their explosives. She was sure they wouldn't risk doing their dirty work in broad daylight.

Mendy started down the trail into the woods, counting her steps as she planned her traps. Yes, she told herself, trapping was the way to go. Mendy had chosen these smaller traps for two reasons: she could handle them alone, and they wouldn't kill or maim the men—just slow them down enough to keep them from getting to the school. It was the only way she could think of to stop them from setting their explosives. If a bomb went off at Highlander while Mrs. Roosevelt was giving her speech, people could get killed. Even Mrs. Roosevelt could get killed. Mendy had to do whatever she could to keep that from happening.

Setting traps takes time and thought. Mendy knew that the element of surprise is what makes traps work best.

The darkness crept around her like a heavy shawl. Every sound caused her to stop and listen. The last thing she needed was to be caught off guard by the Klan.

Mendy decided to set a few traps only a little way into the forest. She grabbed the shovel and dug three shallow holes, spaced a few yards apart along the trail. She was glad the dirt was sandy in this part of woods, but even so, it was hard digging because her shovel kept hitting embedded rocks. When she was done digging, Mendy set the smaller steel traps into the holes and spread leaves and grass over them. In the dark, an unsuspecting person would step into the hole, spring the sharp trap, and fall. He would surely twist a knee or sprain an ankle.

Farther along the trail, she set up the rope trap she had invented herself. She cut four lengths of rope. She tied two of them side by side between two trees, so that the ropes stretched across the trail about five feet high. She tied the other two pieces of rope so they stretched below the first, close to the ground. If a man hit either set of ropes, he'd trip and stumble—right into a modified Victor double four-and-a-half long-spring trap with sharp steel teeth. That ought to slow him down.

Mendy set two more rope traps even farther down the trail. These ropes she set at slightly different levels. When the lower ropes snapped together, they would cut a man's legs awful good. And he would be bound to fall into the shallow hole Mendy had carefully dug for her prey.

When she was done, Mendy paused. By the position of the moon and stars, she knew that several hours had passed. She had almost reached the point where the trail descended down the bluff to the pond and the school lawn. Only the two largest steel traps were left in her wagon. These she planned to set close to the school buildings. They would be the last line of defense. A man caught in one of the steel fox traps would be hard pressed to get up and run.

According to the flyer that Daddy had shown her, Mrs. Roosevelt would be speaking outdoors. Mendy knew the place—an open area between the main building and the pond. Mendy made her way carefully down the bluff. She paused and listened hard. Sounds of night filled the hot air, but she heard no footsteps or voices behind her.

In the last patch of woods that faced Mrs. Roosevelt's speaking place, Mendy searched until she found two abandoned wells she'd discovered along the trail last summer. Only a few boards covered each opening. Mendy tugged at the nails securing the boards, her arms and legs paining her, until she pried the boards up. She threw a few rocks into the wells to check how deep they were. Each time, a hollow thud reached her ears as the rock hit bottom. Mendy was satisfied. The wells were deep enough, but not too deep. Now it was time to find briars and thorns.

The traps Mendy planned were painful ones for the hunter as well as the hunted. She was glad to have the work gloves to protect her hands from the long, sharp thorns, but her arms were cut and bleeding long before the wells were filled. By the time she was done, a good two hours had passed. Around her, the nighttime creatures had quieted. The woods were hushed. Dawn was not far off.

Quickly, Mendy tied a rope low to the ground just in front of each briar-filled well, stretching from one tree to another. Finally, in front of the last well, she tied one more length of rope low to the ground, securing it to only one tree. If by chance some of the men made it through all the other traps, Mendy herself would yank up this rope to ensure they fell into the last hole. The well was deep, and the briars were sharp as knives. There'd be no way a man could climb out.

Mendy hid herself in the bushes nearby, holding the end of the rope loosely in her hand. While she waited, she thought about Mrs. Eleanor Roosevelt and tried to keep her mind off the Klan. Grandma had told her many times, ain't no reason for a sane person to think about evil more than they think about good. And Mendy Anna Thompson was as sane as they come.

As Mendy waited patiently for the light of morning to filter through the trees, she began to doze. The rope slowly dropped from her closed fist. Mendy dreamed of Mr. Hare.

A rustle in the bushes startled Mendy awake. She grabbed the rope and strained to listen. *Probably just a coon snacking on berries,* she thought.

Then Mendy heard a thud. She twisted her body slowly in the direction of the sound, careful not to make any noise herself. Shadows pranced in and out among the trees. Mendy knew they might be merely the shadows of dawn playing tricks. She listened, fighting to slow her breathing. Her heart pounded furiously in her chest.

Then she heard it: something moving steadily through the trees. Mendy's daddy had taught her to distinguish the sounds of animals, birds, and people in the woods. There was no doubt, this was not an animal or a bird. These were footfalls on leaves—a person. Someone had avoided the other traps. Whoever it was, he was not limping but walking steady.

Mendy wrapped the rope around her hand and grasped it tightly. She waited.

The person moved swiftly through the woods, coming from the direction Mendy knew he'd have to come from. Whoever it was, to have gotten this far he must be either a good hunter or plain lucky.

The footsteps came closer. Mendy held her breath, prepared to pull the rope across the path if she needed to. Suddenly Mendy heard someone whispering her name. "Mend. Mend. I know you're in here." It was Jeffrey.

Jeffrey. Of course. Mendy was angry and relieved at the same time. He knew her traps, her secrets. She'd taught him all of them but the secret of the briar traps.

"Where are you?" Jeffrey asked.

Mendy could see him turning around, looking for her. "Don't be mad, Mend. Aunt Sis told me she thought you came here to try to stop the Klan."

Mendy hissed, "I want you to leave now."

"I came to help you," Jeffrey said. "What I said yesterday was wrong, Mend. I'm sorry." He took a step forward on the trail.

"Stop. Stop right there, Jeffrey." One more step and he might trip on the first set of ropes.

Jeffrey stood still. "Where are you?" he asked again.

Just then a crash and swearing sounded through the woods. Someone had hit a trap farther back on the trail. It sounded like the steel fox trap.

Mendy squeezed out of her hiding place. She jumped up and whispered to Jeffrey, "Follow me. Be careful. There might be more than one of 'em." They hurried back along the trail and scrambled up the bluff.

Then Mendy saw it—a rifle lying on the trail. A few feet from it, halfway in the bushes, was a man. He was on his side, tugging frantically at the steel trap on his ankle. Blood stained his pants leg. Mendy could see he'd hit the trap, but he must have come down in an awkward position or hit a sharp rock. His ankle looked broken.

When he caught sight of Mendy, he tried to drag himself over to the rifle, the trap still clamped on his ankle. "I'll kill you, you little nigger," he said. His face twisted as he struggled to reach the rifle. His fingers splayed out, and beads of sweat poured from his reddened face. "Just you wait, nigger."

Jeffrey shouted, "Don't you ever call her that." He dove for the rifle.

Mendy heard the snap of a trap closing on Jeffrey's hand. Her body jerked involuntarily.

Mendy ran to Jeffrey and pulled with all her strength to release the trap. Jeffrey yanked his hand free with a groan and cradled it in his other hand.

In that second, Mendy spotted two things out of the corner of her eye — the glint of a big silver ring with a triangle-shaped stone, and the barrel of a rifle in mid-air.

"Get ready to die, nigger," the man growled. He had managed to stand, and he was lifting the rifle awkwardly to his chin to aim.

Mendy moved her hand to the hilt of the hunting knife at her belt. She knew she couldn't throw it at him. She just couldn't throw a knife directly at a person. But maybe if she threw it hard toward the tree to his right, he'd flinch just enough for her to get away. She gripped the hilt as he raised his rifle.

Mendy could see the man grimacing, sweat running down into his eyes. He shook his huge head like a dog, squinting as beads of water rolled down. It was her chance. She whipped the knife from her belt and threw it straight at the tree. The knife pounded the target and dropped to the ground.

The man with the rifle had flinched as she'd expected. But then the exertion and pain must have doubled him over, and he dropped the rifle.

Mendy knew she should run, but before she could move, Mr. Whitehall—Jeffrey's pa—stepped out onto the trail and stood next to the slumped-over man. Mendy stood very still, barely breathing. His shotgun was aimed directly at her.

"Pa," Jeffrey said, sniffling, tears running down his face. "That man was gonna shoot Mend."

"Be quiet, son," Mr. Whitehall said. "Don't nobody make a move."

Mendy's heart pounded furiously.

"Who hurt you, son?" Mr. Whitehall asked.

Jeffrey grimaced, but he didn't say anything.

"Did you hear me? Who did this?" his father demanded.

"I did it," Jeffrey said. "I set the trap and forgot where I put it."

Mendy shook all over. She was surprised to hear her own voice. "I did it. I didn't mean it for Jeffrey, sir," she said. "It was meant for the Klan." As she spoke, she realized those might be the last words she'd ever say. And the only thought that came floating to her mind was that she hoped—with all her heart—that God would forgive these men.

Mr. Whitehall shouted again, "I said don't move, dadgummit."

Mendy froze, trying to stop trembling.

"Lower your weapon, or I'm going to blow your stinking head off," Mr. Whitehall growled. His eyes seemed to look right at Mendy, but she had no weapon. "Now! Do it now," Mr. Whitehall said. "And get out from behind that tree."

Mendy heard movement behind her, heard a rough voice mutter, "All right, all right."

She was too scared to look around. She glanced over at Jeffrey, who had sunk to the ground and was now gazing past Mendy.

"You nigger-lovers gonna get it when the rest of our brothers get here," the man behind her said. Mendy recognized Mr. Benefield's voice. His hatred cut into her heart like a knife.

"Well, you're wrong," Mr. Whitehall said. "Throw that gun down and kick it over toward me. Benefield, the only brothers you'll see will be on the chain gang. Nobody's coming for you but the sheriff."

Jeffrey yelled, "Pa, the sheriff's in on it."

"It's all right, son," Mr. Whitehall said, never taking his eyes from Mr. Benefield and picking up the rifle. "I've got the sheriff from Memphis on his way here."

"Where's the rest of the Klan, Pa?" Jeffrey asked.

"Ain't no others coming, son. Now, Mendy, see if you can help Jeffrey up and take him with you to Highlander's main house. Somebody's waiting for the sheriff up there. Just tell the sheriff where the rest of your traps are, Mendy.

You two wait up at the school for me. See if somebody can't take care of your hand, son."

Mendy helped Jeffrey up. She said, "Thank you, Mr. Whitehall." And then she whispered, "Thank you, too, Jeffrey."

Mendy wrapped her arms around Jeffrey's waist and helped him along the trail. When they reached the yard near Highlander's main house, a man came running out to meet them. He grabbed Jeffrey and directed Mendy to the sheriff and two deputies. Mendy told the sheriff where to find Mr. Whitehall and the Klansmen and warned him about the remaining traps. She watched him and his men set off through the woods.

❧

About fifteen minutes later, Mr. Whitehall came out of the trees and walked toward Mendy and Jeffrey. Jeffrey's hand had been bandaged, and he and Mendy were sitting out in the yard. "You did the right thing, son. I'm glad you decided to stick up for your friend."

Jeffrey's face was full of confusion. "But, Pa, I don't understand what happened. *Are* you a part of the Klan?"

Mendy didn't know if she could stand this. She got up to move away.

"Wait, Mendy," Mr. Whitehall said, "I want to talk to you, too."

Mendy sat back down, still refusing to look into
Mr. Whitehall's blue eyes.

"Mendy, that was a brave thing you did," Mr. Whitehall
said. "I'm proud of you both. No, Jeffrey, I ain't a member
of the Klan. I've been pretending to be in order to get
information to help stop them. In fact, that's why the
other Klansmen ain't here—last night I told them that
the FBI knew about their plan to bomb Highlander.
Of course, they don't know it was me who told the FBI."
Mr. Whitehall smiled grimly.

"But I couldn't find *those* two men last night," he continued, jerking his thumb back toward the woods. "I didn't
think they'd carry out the raid, just the two of them. But
then last night I heard you sneaking out, Jeffrey, with a
horse, and I was so afraid that somehow the Klan had
gotten to you. They're good at filling young people with
their poison. I should have known you better." He put
a hand on his son's shoulder. "Anyway, Jeffrey, I saw you
was heading toward Monteagle, and I followed you in
my truck. If you hadn't come out to these woods to help
Mendy, I wouldn't have gotten here in time to stop those
two men.

"And, Mendy," Mr. Whitehall went on, "I had no idea
you were such a fine trapper. Jeffrey always talked about
how you can trap as good as a man, and now I guess I'll
have to agree with him. You did a brave thing. And it
mattered more than you know. Turns out those two men

weren't just going to bomb the school. If they'd missed getting Mrs. Roosevelt that way, they planned to shoot her on her way to the airport tonight. You saved her life, young woman."

Mendy looked into his eyes and smiled.

Jeffrey's pa had someone drop Mendy off at Aunt Sis's place, and someone else drove Tandy home with the dray. Aunt Sis had good news for Mendy. Uncle Steven had stopped by to say Mendy's daddy was doing better and he and Mama would be home in a few days. Mendy cried with relief. She explained to Aunt Sis what had happened in the woods. Aunt Sis said she was truly proud of Mendy. Then Mendy got cleaned up, lay down on her pallet, and slept. A few hours later, Mr. Whitehall came by to pick her up.

Soon Mendy was standing on the front lawn of the Highlander Folk School beside Jeffrey and his father, waiting for Mrs. Roosevelt to speak. There were sixty or more people out on the lawn, coloreds and whites, milling around, chatting, some even hugging one another. Mr. Myles Horton was on the porch, seated behind a table, along with some other people. They had decided to let Mrs. Roosevelt speak from the porch, where she would be more protected.

Mendy was so excited and nervous that she wasn't talking at all. When Mrs. Roosevelt came out on the porch and stood at the microphone, wearing a simple dress much like Mendy's mama's dresses and a tiny hat that looked sort of like a turtle, Mendy just wanted to shout.

She listened to every single word Mrs. Roosevelt said. But most of all, she loved it when Mrs. Roosevelt said, "It is wonderful to meet here as people—not as white people and colored people, but just people."

After Mrs. Roosevelt finished her speech, Jeffrey's father had a surprise for Mendy. He led Mendy right up to Mrs. Roosevelt and said, "Here is the young woman I told you about. She is as brave as you are, Mrs. Roosevelt. My son tells me her middle name is Anna, after you."

Mendy glanced over at Jeffrey, remembering how she'd imagined herself, Grandma, and Anna Eleanor Roosevelt riding on the backs of elephants together at the Taj Mahal.

Jeffrey smiled back at Mendy and squeezed her shoulder.

"I am so honored to meet you, young lady," Mrs. Roosevelt said, grasping Mendy's hand in both of hers. "Miss Mendy Anna Thompson, thank you for saving my life." Then she gave Mendy a warm hug and added, "Yes, my dear friend, I'm honored to meet such a brave young woman."

It was a moment Mendy would never forget.

A PEEK INTO THE PAST

LOOKING BACK: 1958

Although Mendy and Jeffrey are fictional, *Circle of Fire* is based on a real incident. Eleanor Roosevelt planned to speak at the Highlander Folk School in Monteagle, Tennessee, on June 17, 1958, to a mixed audience of blacks and whites. Local Ku Klux Klan members, however, despised Highlander and Mrs. Roosevelt for their stand against racism and wanted to disrupt her visit. Some Klansmen even plotted to blow up the school.

The Monteagle sheriff knew about the plot, but like many Southerners in the 1950s, he shared the Klan's beliefs. He told the Klan members he would not stop them from carrying out their plot.

Unknown to the Klan, an FBI informant was attending their meetings and reporting their plans to the FBI, just as Jeffrey's father does in the story. The FBI warned the sheriff that he had to protect Mrs. Roosevelt and the Highlander School. When Klan leaders learned that the FBI knew what was going on, they must have dropped their plans, for Mrs. Roosevelt's speech took place without disruption.

Eleanor Roosevelt speaking at the Highlander Folk School in 1958

In *Circle of Fire,* the author imagines what might have happened if two young people had learned of the Klan's plot and tried to foil it. Although the story is fiction, many of the situations Mendy faces were a real part of life in the rural South.

Like most southern towns in the 1950s, Cowan was *segregated,* or racially divided—not only by custom but by law. Race laws, called *Jim Crow laws,* forbade African Americans to eat at the same restaurants as white people, use the same waiting rooms, live in the same neighborhoods, hold the same jobs, or go to the same schools. Marriage between the races was outlawed, and many people believed it was wrong for a black girl of Mendy's age to be friends with a white boy.

In the mid-1950s, African Americans began to challenge the Jim Crow laws.

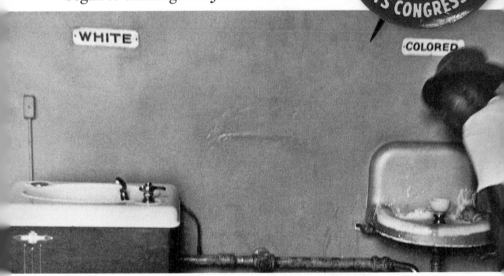

In the 1950s, even drinking fountains were segregated.

Black leaders said it wasn't right that black children's schools were short of books and teachers while white schools had plenty. It wasn't right that black people were made to stand in the back of a bus while whites sat in the front. Some of these legal challenges went all the way to the U.S. Supreme Court, and during the 1950s and 1960s, the race laws came to an end.

Changing people's actions and beliefs, however, proved even harder than changing the laws. Some white people who opposed equal rights for blacks joined the Ku Klux Klan, a group founded after the Civil War. Klan members

used violence to silence black people and their supporters. As Mendy discovers, Klan members met secretly at night, wearing white robes and hoods to hide their identity. At these meetings, they planned raids to beat people up, burn crosses in front of homes or black churches, plant bombs, or even commit murder. Often, town authorities knew about the Klan's activities, but they looked the other way and didn't press charges.

A Ku Klux Klan meeting

Sometimes they even took part in Klan raids themselves.

Not all white people shared the Klan's views, but very few stood up against the Klan. Like Mendy's and Jeffrey's mothers, they knew that actions which drew the Klan's attention could be dangerous. A few brave people did work to stop the Klan. Some, like Jeffrey's father in the story, secretly reported on the Klan to the FBI.

Myles Horton took another approach. He believed education was the best way to change people's views, so he founded the Highlander Folk School for adults of all races in 1932. At first Highlander focused on helping miners and other workers improve their working conditions. By the 1950s, the school was one of the few places in the nation where people could study ways of improving race relations. Horton hired a black woman to organize the school's workshops—a bold step at the time.

At Highlander, blacks and whites came together to discuss problems, share experiences, and just plain get to know each other. One of the most important things people learned at Highlander was how to stand up for

Myles Horton and the Highlander Folk School in Monteagle, Tennessee

Children swimming together at Highlander

Highlander students enjoying each other's company

their rights peacefully but effectively. Black civil rights leaders such as Martin Luther King, Jr., and Andrew Young attended the school. So did Rosa Parks, a young black woman whose refusal to move to the back of a bus in Montgomery, Alabama, launched the civil rights movement in 1955—only a few months after she had studied at Highlander.

Rosa Parks in the 1950s

Simply visiting the school could be risky, especially for blacks. But Highlander had a powerful supporter: former First Lady Eleanor Roosevelt.

Mrs. Roosevelt, widow of President Franklin D. Roosevelt, believed strongly that all Americans deserved equal rights. She spoke and wrote eloquently in support of African Americans, and she showed her beliefs by her actions. The incident that Mendy's father describes from his army days, for example, when Mrs. Roosevelt shared a black soldier's ice cream cone, is true. In the 1950s, racism ran so deep that the idea of a white person sharing a black person's food seemed unthinkable, so when the former First Lady herself performed this small act, it had a powerful effect. Such actions earned Mrs. Roosevelt enormous respect among African Americans.

The fight against segregation was not popular in 1958,

especially in the South, but the support of someone as famous and respected as Eleanor Roosevelt made people reconsider the issue— exactly what the Klan and their sympathizers were afraid of.

Mrs. Roosevelt greeting black soldiers abroad

Although the Klan did not stop Mrs. Roosevelt's speech, a year later the state of Tennessee shut down the Highlander School, hoping to end its influence. But Myles Horton knew that his work was too important to give up, and he later reopened the school in Knoxville, Tennessee. Although the Highlander School is not widely known, it had a profound effect on race relations and civil rights in the United States. In 1982, Highlander was nominated for a Nobel Peace Prize for its historic role in educating people about human rights.

Highlander today, in Knoxville, Tennessee

AUTHOR'S NOTE

We all owe our gratitude to the people of the Highlander Research and Education Center (formerly the Highlander Folk School) for their continued tireless effort on behalf of every citizen of the United States. In addition, I owe a large debt to the Highlander librarian, Juanita Householder, and other Highlander staff.

I could not have written this book without the assistance of Joseph Lujan of Cowan, Tennessee, and his firsthand knowledge of Mrs. Roosevelt's visit to Highlander; and Dr. Scott Bates, a retired professor at the University of the South, who shared his stories about Myles Horton and also participated in the first lawsuit aimed against segregation in the area. Thank you both for walking with me through the old Highlander grounds and sharing your memories. Thanks also to Dora Turner and Ms. (Sis) Swain for telling me about the trains and rolling stores.

I cannot put into words the gratitude I feel to Guy and Candie Carawan for their willingness to share not only their knowledge but their home with a total stranger. Their music and words will forever live in my heart. What a night of fireworks!

Thanks to Troy Fore, editor of *The Speedy Bee,* a beekeeping newspaper, for helping me keep my story straight.

Thanks also to the real Calvin Johnson for telling someone his Eleanor Roosevelt ice cream story. I read about it in the book *The Candle She Lit: A Woman of Quality, Eleanor Roosevelt,* by Stella K. Hershan.

Finally, thanks to Ernest and Jackie Varner for giving me a place to stay while writing this book.

ABOUT THE AUTHOR

Evelyn Coleman is the author of another History Mystery, *Mystery of the Dark Tower,* and several award-winning books for children and young adults.

Writing *Circle of Fire* was a very personal experience for her. Evelyn, like Mendy, grew up in the South during the 1950s, when racial segregation was the law. Like Mendy, she was raised with stories of Eleanor Roosevelt's courageous stand for equal rights. And, like Mendy, she had a close friend who was white—but sadly, Evelyn's friendship ended because of racism.

Here is what she would like to tell readers about that friendship and about *Circle of Fire:*

> *One of my close childhood friends was Carla. She lived on the opposite end of our street. We played together almost every day until I was about twelve years old. That fall, Carla decided it was no longer okay for us to*

play together. At that time, it still had not occurred to me that there was a problem being friends with her because she was white and I was black. My parents explained that the other white children who had moved onto the street (and had refused to play with me) had possibly persuaded Carla that it wasn't a good idea to be close friends with a "colored" girl.

I was so hurt when I lost her as a friend. It took me many years to get over that experience. My hope is that no children are judged by things like race, culture, or ethnic group, but by their character. I believe that it is important to read and learn about all *cultures, not just your own—that it will help us all live in an improved world.*

As you read this story, I hope you will remember that "hate" is always dangerous. And that it is important to speak out when you see something wrong.

And Carla, I miss you still.

Request a Catalogue

Welcome to a world that's all yours—because it's filled with the things girls love! Beautiful dolls that capture your heart. Books that send your imagination soaring. And games and pastimes that make being a girl great!

For your free **AmericanGirl®** catalogue, return this postcard, call 1-800-845-0005, or visit our Web site at americangirl.com

Send me a catalogue:

Name_____ Address_____

City_____ State_____ Zip_____

Girl's birth date___/___/___ Parent's signature_____
           month day year
❑ Work phone (   ) _____ E-mail address_____
❑ Home phone

12583i

Send my friend a catalogue:

Name_____ Address_____

City_____ State_____ Zip_____

12591i

Get a risk-FREE preview issue!

American Girl® magazine— especially for girls 8 and up

Mail this card to get a risk-FREE preview issue of *American Girl* magazine and start your one-year trial subscription. If you like *American Girl*, you'll receive 5 more bimonthly issues (6 total) for only $19.95! If not, just return the invoice marked "cancel." The preview issue is yours to keep—FREE.

Send bill to: (please print)

_____
Adult's name

_____
Address

Send magazine to: (please print)

_____ ___/___
Girl's name   Birth date

_____
Address

_____
City   State   Zip

_____
City   State   Zip

_____
Adult's signature

Guarantee: You may cancel at any time for a full refund. Allow 4–6 weeks for first issue. Canadian subscription $24 U.S., prepaid only.

K14L1

American Girl ®

PO BOX 620497
MIDDLETON WI 53562-0497

BUSINESS REPLY MAIL

FIRST-CLASS MAIL   PERMIT NO. 190   BOONE IA

POSTAGE WILL BE PAID BY ADDRESSEE

AmericanGirl ®

PO BOX 37311
BOONE IA 50037-2311